Losing Faith

NORA CALDER

First published in March 2016 by Nora Calder

This edition published in Northern Ireland in 2017
by Excalibur Press

ISBN: 978-1-910728-46-8

Formatting & layout by
Excalibur Press

Excalibur Press
Belfast, Northern Ireland

team@excaliburpress.co.uk
07982628911 | @ExcaliburPress
www.excaliburpress.co.uk

www.noracalder.co.uk

For PCB, My OneLove

CHAPTER 1

I've never failed a test, never scored less than top marks and certainly never been asked to repeat an assignment, I was almost going to ask for a re-mark but I relented. It's Monday afternoon and I've slumped into the snug brown leather sofa in Harmony, my favourite coffee shop. Though, I feel anything but harmonious. Adele's new hit Hello is echoing around the place and I sit singing to myself while sipping on my caramel latte with an extra shot, intended to force my brain into work mode, though today it is failing miserably.

I try not to stare at the vacant screen on my MacBook as seeing it only melts my head further, instead I admire the vintage décor that the owner Sandra has chosen. White sanded tables and elegant white and silver walls, topped with a smooth light grey wooden floor. This place is my haven. I always come here when I have work to do and most days I get a lot done, not today. My brain refuses to function at my increasingly frustrated command. I have too much on my mind; I'm getting lost in this song and distracted by intrusive thoughts.

"I can turn that down if it's distracting you." That rasping American tone cuts through my distraction, I feel electrified. My cheeks begin to heat up; I know oh too well my face will be getting redder by the second.
I raise my head, smiling faintly at the new barista.
"I don't mind, I like the distraction, well I don't. I mean I need to get this essay done but no you don't have to do that." I laugh nervously. In fact, I've been far more sidetracked by the

4

new barista for the past hour than I have been by anything else. I've been studying every move, listening to every word and becoming almost infatuated. Maybe I'm just forcing myself to think about anything other than my essay, well at least that's what I tell myself. I should really leave. The barista laughs back, smiling sweetly.

"Well maybe a top up?" That voice is like a purr. "Nah I'm okay I'm gonna go now anyway." I sit forward, close my laptop with a thud and squeeze it into my bag, swigging down the last of my caramel latte, I stand looking intently into those piercing blue eyes that I've been dying to get the attention of ever since I walked in here today, yet as soon as I have them the guilt is repulsing me. I could almost vomit all over Sandra's lustrous grey floor.

"Hey Babe, you leavin?" Gregg appears from behind the barista, snapping me out of this uncomfortable mind-set and throwing me into an equally uncomfortable yet polar opposite mindset, he lands a peck on my lips.

"Hey, yea I'm so sorry I've gotta get home, need my notes for this essay, I meant to text you." If only my boyfriend could see with X-ray vision into my bag he would know it's loaded with enough notes to write 1000 essays.

"No bother Faith, I'll see you at the Bible Study tonight sure?" He smiles brightly he clearly hasn't got a clue what's going on behind my fake smile.

"If I get this finished, I'll be there, promise, I'll see you later." I give Gregg half a dry kiss on the cheek whilst focusing on the Barista's deep enchanting eyes. I squeeze inelegantly past him as he stands looking slightly dumbfounded and catch the eye of the barista who breaks eye contact to clean an already clean table.

I can feel both of their eyes following me as I rush outside; I embrace the cold air and take a much needed deep breath. My heart pumps swiftly inside my chest and I feel close to a full blown panic attack. The tears stream down my face and sting me with the bitter cold, I have a crushing sense of self-loathing and shame that I can't shake the whole tearful drive home.

***

My knees rest on the thick spongy grey carpet beneath them, elbows pressed on top of my bed, tears rush down my face like a fast moving river soaking my bright pink duvet with the words 'Sweet Dreams' printed in bold grey letters. It's been a long time since I've had sweet dreams. I enter a state of complete desperation as I cry out to God, imploring him to please help me, to reach out and touch my mind, set me free. The front door closes, my parents return from the Bible study, every Monday evening from as far back as I remember they have attended like clockwork.

I scrape my now trembling body off the floor and slip under the cold duvet pulling it over my head, both for the heat and to feel like I'm concealed from the world. I rest in the foetal position, trying to bring myself a little relief. My humid breath heats my face as it hits the duvet, the tears are showing no signs of giving up as they soak my duck feather filled pillow. My body convulses as I sob uncontrollably struggling to catch a much needed breath. What is wrong with me? I just want to feel normal. God make me normal.

***

I stretch my rigid body in my seemingly roasting bed, pawing underneath my pillows to locate my Iphone which is sporting a wrecked screen thanks to an unwanted trip I took down the garden path. I really must get that fixed, if I ever find the time. The light beams off my eyes like the sun as I turn the brightness on my phone to its minimum and let out a relieving sigh. 2:56AM. I can remember crying profusely for hours, I can only assume that I exhausted my body and mind to sleep. I jerk upright on the bed. "Ahh, my essay," I say out loud, realising I've completely abandoned it the day before it's due to be submitted. I've also deserted Gregg, 4 text and 3 missed calls prove that. I should have contacted him but he was the least of my worries, though guilt is my most featured emotion these days so I allow it to kick in with no hesitations. I send him a quick message telling him I fell asleep and that I'll see him tomorrow night at church. The prayer meeting is every Tuesday night, another must attend service, my parent's love it and I've been going with them for years except when I have an assignment due, only then do they accept my reasons for not attending.

I have given myself no alternative, I must bury myself in my essay for a solid number of hours in order to get it finished and I need to make sure I pass this time, my determination kicks in and I begin to type heartily. I'm lucky that tonight the words are flowing, other times, like earlier I could sit for hours and not write a single word. My safe-haven bedroom probably has some impact on that, three of my walls are brilliant white with the feature wallpapered with miniature floral designs in all the shades of pink you can imagine. On the feature wall hangs a bulky vertical Mirror with grey outline, I seldom use this mirror as it's really just for show. Another wall has hundreds of black and white photos of my family, Gregg,

Shannon and other friends from church. All of this matches wonderfully with my white wooden bedroom furniture that I spent hours debating over in Ikea, thank goodness for the hotdog after that trip, it was like a trophy, well done for surviving our maze.

CHAPTER 2

Tuesday morning, 8am and I feel absolutely elated, even though my sleeping pattern now resembles that of an owl, they are one of my favourite animals but I'd rather not have to cover the bags under my eyes with heavy foundation. My essay is finished; I got it emailed off just before the deadline. The Bible says, 'I can do all things through Christ who strengthens me,' I give God the credit for the achievement as I've been trained to do all my life. I've decided this morning in my resolute mind-set that I need to get on top of life and not let it get on top of me, balancing my studies with church, family and Gregg, it may be a bumpy ride but I'll get there in the end. I say a prayer to that effect, and bury my unwanted thoughts far below the surface of my perfect Christian persona as I do so.

I stand in front of my full length mirror which is strategically located on the inside of my wardrobe door in order that it doesn't look like clutter. I straighten my lengthy ash blonde hair, dyed of course, and admire my new Jack Wills jacket that I treated myself to or rather my parents treated me to, anyway, it's a bright shade of Navy with Pink writing and I've been wanting it for ages. I complete my outfit with tight blue

skinny jeans which hug my toned figure and bright white converse. I feel tranquil today and my image reflects that. I'm not used to this amount of makeup but my skin is tired today. I normally get away with minimal foundation as I'm quite swarthy and I find a lot of makeup makes me break out in spots, my only two essentials are my Chanel eyebrow pencil and my Maybelline Rose coloured lipstick.

I believe in the power of prayer and I know God listened to me last night, I feel a sense of freedom. My Mum barely knocks my door as she strides in, still in her pink fluffy dressing gown, she's around 5ft3, the same height as me, and she's also opted to dye her hair blonde. Mum has given me her green eyes which I like; she always has a face full of makeup and dresses in expensive clothing, going to the gym regularly to ensure she stays in shape.

"Have you got classes today Faith?" Mum asks raising an eyebrow at me.

"No Mum, I've just emailed my essay off there, I'm meeting Shannon for coffee, what's that look for?" I give her a bemused look, though I know too well what the raised eyebrow is for.

"Okay love, try and make the prayer meeting tonight, everyone was asking for you last night. It's those shoes you wear, I told you they're sight but you never listen," shaking her head judgmentally.

"I'll be there Mum don't worry, I'm looking forward to it and everyone wears these shoes," I moan. Maybe I'd be better dressing from her wardrobe then she might not feel the need to comment on my appearance every day.

***

Shannon is sauntering through my door as I get down the cream carpeted stairs my Mum is obsessed with keeping clean.

"Hey wee love," I draw out jokingly. "Come on you, I'm dyin for a cupppaaaa."

Shannon drags out comically. I swallow hard, knowing full

well where she wants to go for coffee.

"Me too, I reckon we should have a wee Starbucks?" I grab my coat from under the stairs. "Shut up! Faith doesn't want to go to harmony? Have you lost the plot?" Shannon chuckles and looks around the hallway confused.

"Is something different?" Shannon asks. The downstairs of the house is designed beautifully; bright white walls with glittering chandelier lights and a broad front door with windows at either side, expensive paintings litter the walls.

My parents are the most house proud people I've ever met.

"No you eejit, someone sent me a snapchat and it put me in the mood for one, aye Mum got rid of the table that used to sit there, she said it was a state," We laugh, both of us know exactly what my Mum is like.

***

Shannon and I push our way through the crowds in the town and arrive at a busy Starbucks. I block out Harmony and anything held within, I don't want to go there today. Shannon offers to get the coffee and I graciously accept, neither of us keep track of who should buy it next but we're out that often that we agree it'll all equal out in the end. She's stood in the line waiting to be served looking over at me with raised brows as if to say, 'You sit there by the window relaxing while I stand in the queue.' I smile widely to tease her. There will be no hard feelings, we've been best friends and next door neighbours our whole lives. We're different in so many ways, Shannon is very girly, she wears a lot of makeup and sports a skirt and top or a dress almost every day, probably how my Mum would like me to dress. She has a curvy figure and all of her clothes are always very flattering, perhaps because she spends hours trawling through the shops and trying all sorts on before she finally parts with her money. Her dark brown hair is scraped back into a messy bun today but she still manages to look fabulous. I always find when I scrape my hair back I look like Miss Trunchbull, though it would need to be after someone pours a litre of bleach over her head. Anyway, I look over at Shannon and I'm proud, she's always dreamed of becoming a nurse and is close to completing her degree, she'll suit it, a caring nature is a must in that profession. She works so hard and contributes so much to the church; sometimes I wish my life was as straightforward as hers.

I look into Shannon's wide brown eyes are she sips over her mocha, her grin noticeable even from behind the mug.
"So, tell me about Gregg?" She asks menacingly. I've been with Gregg since high school but Shannon still feels the need to ask me this every time we have coffee, as if one day something substantial will have changed. Gregg is the son of Pastor Leacher the radical leader of the Pentecostal Church I attend, both he and his wife adore Gregg and his Brother Harry. My man is around 6ft4. He plays rugby which gives him an incredibly sculpted muscular build. He has short brown hair which always seems to sit perfectly, he says he just combs it but I'm sure he uses a bit of hairspray at times.

"We're all good Shannon, he's working away at the youth work and we see each other as much as we can, between University, work and Church it's a bit of a nightmare getting time alone." I smile but let out a small inward sigh as I knock back my caramel latte.
"Well, he's a keeper Faith, I've always said that, tall dark and handsome, I wish Harry wasn't taken." She laughs. Shannon is always on the hunt for a man, she's desperate to get married,

have kids and be the perfect Christian homemaker.

Shannon and I have been sitting for hours and I feel I am nearing a caffeine overdose. We've been catching up on University drama and then ended on the topic we are both constantly enmeshed in; church and the entire goings on, upcoming events and commitments that we need to follow through on. Shannon is so passionate about church life and I love that about her. If I'm having a bad day she is able to encourage me and pick me up, she always has an inspirational Bible verse at the tip of her tongue.

Shannon tells me about the new guy she's been getting to know, the whole time my mind is somewhere else though and I feel guilty for not listening to my best friend. Instead I've allowed my head to wander into Harmony; I'm watching that new barista all over again. Maybe one day I'll build up the bravery to tell my best friend about the crazy thoughts I've been hiding away for so long. Though it's unlikely, I know Shannon would be disgusted and ashamed of me and rightly so.

CHAPTER 3

"As we battle through these last days Lord let us draw strength from you, let us pursue your word and be servants of the living God. The world is full of sin and perversion and let us spread your hope to those heading for an eternity of damnation Lord. In your precious name. Amen. Say Amen with me."

I lift my head despairingly, gazing up at the stage, our church the King's Presence Worship Centre is huge, it seats around 600 people, it is lined with rows of contemporary soft blue chairs, to match the blue and gold carpet, the walls are white and filled with posters bearing inspirational words. 'If God be for us, who could be against us?' is the one my eyes are always drawn to. We have a full band, singers, drummers, bass guitar players; it's far from the hymn singing, full of the elderly place that most people expect when they hear the word church. Pastor Leacher brings to a close the hour and thirty minute prayer meeting and I'm not hanging around for a chat, I am dead beat, all of that coffee today and now I'm crashing.

"Mummy, I'm heading on, Gregg and I are going to watch a film and then I need an early night." I give my mum a hug and wave at my Dad who is already chatting away to his church friends. My Dad's tall and has a stocky build, he goes to the gym like Mum and I'm sure he uses just for men on his dark brown hair to conceal his silver streaks, he's always finely dressed in high-priced suits and most likely spends more money on his shoes than Mum does. He's the ideal family man at church, everyone looks up to him, he does a lot for them and Pastor Leacher treats him like a brother, his 10% tithes unquestionably amount to a lot each week but I'm sure that has nothing to do with it.

Gregg takes my hand in the car park and walks me to my shiny white Vauxhall Corsa that my parents bought me for starting university. I slump into the seat.
"I'm so tired babe," I yawn as I start the engine, switching the radio off, I'm too tired to listen to music, it's bizarre, but I am.
"I won't stay for long, I've missed you." Gregg grins, his luminous white teeth stealing my attention. My boyfriend is so perfect, incredibly handsome, tanned skinned and sports a rugged stubble look today. He has the most incredibly brown eyes, with long dark eyelashes that any woman would envy, including me. I love his enthusiasm for his job, helping disadvantaged youth and one day he wants to have his own youth centre, my parents respect him and in their minds he is perfect for me.

I change into my comfy navy and white snowflake Pyjamas and hop into bed, the fleece always ends up being torn off in the middle of the night when I wake sweating from the heat but it will do for now.
"Your Da's not gonna kick me out of your room again is he?" Gregg asks fretfully as he sits on the edge of my bed.
"Babe I told you, he was in a foul mood that day, they won't be back for a few hours anyway, they always stay for tea and buns after every meeting, you know my Mum, she's scared of missing something." Gregg laughs at my words knowingly. Ordinarily we go to Gregg's place to chill out together, my Dad scared me one day, he bust in when we were lying in bed, fully clothed, may I add. I know if he was here there's no way he'd allow this but I keep that to myself knowing Gregg will

be gone when they return.

I haven't spent time alone with Gregg for what feels like ages and I can't help but blame myself for that. Sometimes I feel like I push the poor guy away and then the guilt sets in and I reel him back in again like a fish caught on a line. We're in love though and we truly try and make sure we live out God's word and that includes no sex before marriage, it's important to him and to me. It's hard not to allow your mind to wander especially when we're alone. Having him in my bed feels odd however I'm pleased, especially given that he's looking his finest tonight. He gets under the covers with me, leaning over and giving me a kiss as I lie on my back. He's so affectionate, I love that about him, my mind digresses to Harmony, that day, me leaving him standing there. Why do I keep thinking about it? I need a distraction my mind is beginning to race and distasteful thoughts are sifting through.

I tug on Gregg's shirt with resolve pulling him down until he's leaning over me, then I raise my head somewhat, kissing his soft lips with meaning. I feel his hand slide down my side and it makes me jolt slightly, as it tickles my skin. It startles Gregg and he lies on his side next to me. "Are you okay?" He asks concerned.
"Of course babe, I just haven't had you to myself in so long," I lean in kissing him again this time a little more roughly sneaking my hand up his shirt, feeling his muscular build, he lets my hands explore him. I allow our kiss to become more heated as I glide my tongue into his warm mouth and then bite on his bottom lip teasingly. Gregg's hand begins to wonder again, my breath quickens and my heart is pumping blood through my body at lightning speed. What has gotten into me, I'm scared and exposed. I don't know if I feel good, I

don't know if I want him touching me anymore. I end our kiss and look into his gorgeous brown eyes, his hand glides further up my vest, I can tell I've got him excited, isn't that what I wanted? It's strange, I do want to have this closeness but my mind is in constant turmoil. I smile and kiss Gregg again closing my eyes and battling off those oh too familiar intrusive thoughts.

Before I know it, I'm pulling Gregg on top of me, we both have our clothes on but things are getting pretty fiery and he starts to grind himself down onto me. I can feel his erection pressing against me but it doesn't feel right, it's because we're sinning, isn't it? He kisses my neck roughly, the sounds of his groans in my ear are horrible and the heat of his breath turns my stomach. His hand runs over my right breast through my bra. This hasn't happened before and I know it's me leading him to sin but I need this intimacy. My mind shoots back and forth like a yoyo, this feels good but it feels bad, I don't want this but I do. I try and stop thinking but my mind only wanders and before I know it, it isn't Gregg on top of me. I gasp piercingly and feel a tear trickle down my face.
"Stop, stop." I whimper.

Gregg leaps off me and off the bed. "I'm sorry we shouldn't, I shouldn't, it's not right, we're not married."
I sit up on my bed, feeling like I could projectile vomit all over him, the weight of the shame for my perverted thoughts is almost feeling too much a burden to carry and now I'm dragging him into it.
"It's not your fault Gregg it was me, my parents will be home soon." I hold myself together not allowing the dam to open and a river of tears to flow, though I can feel them building with the lump in my throat. Gregg grabs his jacket.

"I'll call you tomorrow." His cheeks are flushed as he leaves my room shaking his head. I roll over into my customary foetal position, body trembling, crying, what is wrong with me? Why can't I just feel normal? I call out to God. "Please take it away God, I know it is evil and it's the devil. Why am I thinking these ghastly thoughts, take them away, just please make it stop God." I don't want to go on feeling this; I'd rather not be here at all than be ensnared with a mind that's driving me insane.

Chapter 4

I wake to the sound of my Dad's Third Day music blasting around the house, I love Christian music, not that I have much of a choice, my Dad won't have anything else being played in the house. I had another restless night, and crying is becoming my favourite past time. After some morning prayers I'm feeling a renewed strength of body and mind. I really have faith in the power of prayer and that's half the battle, if you don't believe you won't receive. I'm doing my obligatory morning check of my phone and Joyce who runs the Sunday school has text me, she's wanting me to help out with an upcoming presentation and I'm happy to consent. At least that will keep my psyche focused for a few weeks, which can only be a good thing. I've no classes this week and I'm feeling creative so I'm eager to get stuck in.

Dad's music is echoing around my large white tiled wet room. I switch on the shower and step cautiously under the hot water, it feels remarkable. Being in the shower always gives me the feeling of washing away my troubles, I remember Pastor Leacher used that as an example in church and it has always stuck with me.

***

"I'm going to Harmony to work on some plans for Sunday school." I call out to my parents as I'm halfway out the door. Not that they'd hear me over the music but it's polite to let them know.

***

I push open the weighty glass door and step into line for my caramel latte, I think I'll omit the extra shot today; Joyce hasn't put a lot of pressure on me, unlike my lecturer.

"I'll have a large caramel latte please." I smile cheerfully.

"No problem Faith, I'll bring it right over." Beams Stephen, he's worked here for years and attends our church though he's very quiet; I don't know much about him. I get my customary station set up, laptop plugged in and ready to kick start my day, I'm feeling productive and I've heaps of ideas for Joyce. I must text Gregg, I haven't replied to his 'I hope you're okay I'm sorry' message last night. I tell Gregg not to worry because I know last night was my fault and not his. I don't want to drag him down again and I won't. I've asked him to come round on his lunch break if he's free, hopefully that'll clear up the embarrassment of last night.

"One Caramel Latte," that soothing American accent startles me and my face shows that. "Sorry I didn't mean to alarm you." The barista chuckles, smiling through perfect lustrous white teeth and showing off the most fine-looking dimples I've ever seen. My cheeks blush a dark shade of pink, I drag myself back into my mind as it tries hard to wander off.

"It's okay." I laugh nervously. My latte is set on the table and a smooth slender hand reaches out to me, I stare at it, then up, then back to the hand. "I guess I'll be seeing a lot of you, I'm Addison." She uses her other hand to tuck her long dark brown hair behind her ear as it hangs from her loose bun. This girl looks like something straight off the catwalk, around 5FT7 with bronzed skin that looks like it's been given a million spa treatments to give it a soft glow. I'm captured by the eyes, bright blue, like the sea in one of those Mexican holiday snaps seen on Instagram.

My heart beats a million beats per minute; I feel my palm sweat, 'Great' I think to myself as I reach for her hand, shaking it.

"I'm Faith." How long have I been shaking her hand? I need to stop. I can't. My face is getting redder. What is wrong with me? What is wrong with her? Addison slips her hand off mine at a snail's pace and I notice tattoos showing at the wrists of her black shirt, she's definitely not the typical barista in Harmony. "So what do you come here to do then Faith apart from to drink coffee and stalk me obviously?" her dry humour is intriguing.

"Today I just have stuff, we'll work to do, well not work, church stuff, work for church, for the Sunday school, they need my help with some stuff, you?" Why have I just asked what she comes here for? Work clearly. Damn. Addison giggles softly.

"I just come here for the view." Her eyes burn on me as she speaks, making my chest rise and fall in deep breaths.

"I'm joking, my Aunt owns this place, I've just moved from New York." Wow, this girl is Sandra's niece, funny I've heard her speak of her sister and niece before.

"Awk how are you finding it then? I've heard Sandra speak about you and your Mum, did she move over too?" The smile on Addison's face gradually fades and she looks at the floor.

"No, My Mom passed away, that kind of sparked the move." Oh no, I knew that, my Mum told me Sandra's sister had passed away, why didn't I remember. How stupid of me. Change the subject Faith.

"I'm really sorry to hear that, Sandra's a good friend of my Mum, if you need shown around or anything you can let me know."

I'm relaxing a little more now in her presence, even though I've landed myself in a bit of a hole but my heart is now only beating at a moderate thousand beats per minute.

"Ah I know now, you're Faith, your Mum is Marj she has invited us over for dinner some night." I sip on my caramel latte, not breaking eye contact with those mysterious eyes as we speak.

"That's good you should come to church sometime too." Addison's laugh is infectious, I wasn't joking but she has certainly taken it that way.

"I've told my Aunt Sandra, if I stepped foot in there, they'd be mopping me off the floor, I'd melt." We both burst out laughing and people close by turn to have a nosey.

"Addison can you clear those tables?" Stephen calls from behind the counter. Her eyes roll as she gives him the thumbs up.

"So are you going to ask me for my number?" My heart sinks and I feel my face return to a beetroot shade.

"What?" I know the confusion and terror is written all over my face.

"You're going to show me around, you'll need my number." The poise is pouring out of her and it is unbelievably alluring.

"Yea of course, I was waiting on you," I try and act confident back, though the shade of my face would say I'm anything but confident or comfortable. Addison scribbles her number down on a napkin and hands me it.

"Now don't turn into a stalker, I have enough of those." Oh

my God, did she just wink at me? Before I know it I'm watching her like a hawk as she clears up some tables, envying her long tempting legs, and that round, stop. These thoughts are abominable, I feel mortified to be in my own mind right now. I silently pray.

"God I know your will for my life, I know that sin is all around me and I know it's disgusting, help me rid my mind of this perversion."

I keep my eyes glued to my MacBook for the next hour hoping Gregg calls round on his lunch but my hope is in vain so I write out the plans for the Sunday school event, making up a flyer to advertise, the more people who come, the more chance to win some souls to Christ. I noticed Addison's shift ending, she gawked over at me as she walked out the door but I pretended not to notice and continued typing. One Small Victory, I guess.

CHAPTER 5

I sit at the breakfast table with Mum, Dad's gone to work and she's made me some scrambled eggs and toast, though she's only having the eggs today, no carbohydrates for her, she's been bad this week apparently. Being bad to her is probably eating both sticks of a Kit-Kat. Mum tells me she's spoken to Pastor Leacher and explained that I'll be finishing University soon but until then I'll be focusing a lot on my study, she said he understood if I didn't get to as many meetings. Well that decision was made for me, I didn't ask Mum to speak to him but I'm sure it's for the best; I don't want to have to repeat another assignment.

Mum begins her morning clean of the already clean house and I lie down on the couch and flick through morning television, nothing interests me. I give Shannon a call and we chat about the guy she's been texting, his name is Gavin and she's hoping to have a date with him soon, though he's in England working at the minute, I really hope it works out for her, she deserves to be happy.

"It's ridiculous that we're on the phone when you could walk 20 steps to my house Faith," Shannon laughs brashly and I can almost hear her from next door.

"I know but I don't want to walk babe, I'm going for a shower anyway, I'll catch you later."

***

Gregg was supposed to come over tonight but he's cancelled, said he has to cover for a colleague who is off sick, that's bad news for me, I was looking forward to seeing him. Shannon is 'busy'; I'm guessing she'll be on the phone to Gavin all evening. Now I'm all dressed up with nowhere to go. Well I wouldn't say I'm dressed up, I'm wearing black skinny jeans with maroon brogues and a matching string vest, hardly dressed for the red carpet. I flick through Facebook hoping something will entertain me, stories of eventful bus journeys and photos of people's dinner are enough to almost bore me to tears.

I'm about to give up on having any plans today when I remember Addison, not that I'd forgotten her, quite the opposite, I just remember I told her I'd show her around. Maybe she'd want to hang out tonight. I give her a text to see if she's free and it gives me butterflies in my stomach when I press send but that's routine when you're getting to know new people, well it is for me, I can be quite timid I think. It's a yes from Addison, though we don't have a plan on where to go, I agree to pick her up in an hour.

I put on my black blazer to match my outfit and fix my make up a bit, well by that I mean slap on an extra layer of lipstick on top of the layer which is wearing off. My parents don't ask where I'm going for once and I don't bother telling them. I sit outside Sandra's house and beep the horn, Sandra comes to the door and waves excitedly at me she's such a charming woman. It's nice that Addison is staying with her; I always think she must be lonely, she's never married and she doesn't have any children either, rumour has it that she's not able to have kids. Though I always thought it was nasty for people to speculate.

Addison gets in the car and the first thing I take in is her perfume, it's intoxicating.

"Wow, you smell great, what is that?" Addison has a proud look on her face, she knows she smells good and she likes that I've said it.

"It's called Black XS all the girls love it." That cackle isn't one you can be silent with and I laugh along with her, even though she's joking about being gay I think, is she gay? I don't know, she probably wouldn't be working at Harmony if she was and she most likely wouldn't be so friendly, from what I hear at church, gay people are the worst sinners of the worst. I can see her tattoos tonight she has her right full arm covered in loads of different designs, I notice some skulls, she's carrying her black leather jacket, wearing a white cotton vest, tucked into black high waist jeans and white converse shoes, we have the same taste in shoes. She has a really cool dress sense and seems to look amazing all the time. Her hair is down and straight tonight which shows its length it goes mid-way down her long curved back.

I start the car and begin to drive, turning the music down so that it plays lowly in the background.

"So, where are you taking me then? I'm excited." That accent is so calming, I could listen to her all day.

"Church," I keep looking ahead, my tone dry. "You're kidding right?" I can tell Addison doesn't know if I'm joking or not.

"No I'm serious I have the mop bucket in the boot." We laugh together at the top of our voices, she pushes my arm playfully, I've only been in her company such a short space of time but I feel in high spirits inside, it's weird, I think she could turn out to be a terrific friend.

"Okay, on a serious note, there's nothing to do in Belfast so," I'm struggling to think of where we can go, with church we always go bowling, ice rink or cinema, that's the height of it. "There must be, don't tell me I've used my good perfume for nothing," she jokes.

"Well we could go bowling?" I utter uneasily, she's likely going to think I'm a loser.

"Yea that would be awesome and I'll whip your ass, not literally, unless you want." My face is the colour of blood instantly, my heart pounds and I feel uncomfortable.

"I'm joking I'm joking, you'll get to know my sense of humour, if you stick around long enough." When Addison laughs, I laugh, most of the time because she's funny or because her laugh is so contagious.

I haven't stopped smiling since Addison got into my car and this doesn't change as we stroll into the bowling alley. It's dimly lit and I like that; anytime Addison makes eye contact with me I feel like my cheeks flush, it's embarrassing; at least in here she won't be able to see so much. "This is my treat," Addison beams as she pays for the both of us.

"Are you sure? I can give you money?" I reply uncomfortably.

"I'm sure, you can pay next time when we go to some fancy restaurant," I giggle at her, looking into those sea blue eyes, there'll be a next time?

"So are you ready to get beat?" I lift my first bowling ball, and hold it up smiling at her. "You may have handled more balls than me but you're definitely losing girl." Addison pouts her lips, waiting for my reaction, it's like she knows that'll make me go red in the face and maybe she likes that.

"I definitely haven't, that's boke." I laugh noisily trying to hide my innocence as I take my shot. I don't even manage a spare, knowing she's watching me puts me under pressure, at least that's my justification anyway. Addison lifts a ball.

"Ready to learn from the master?" that confidence, it's so endearing; she says things but keeps her face straight then gives a small grin. With that Addison lands a strike, her smile is wide and I can tell she's super competitive. "Did I mention I have a sore finger? That's why I'm not at my best?" I joke, trying to break through the mile long ice that is stopping me from relaxing around this girl.

"Really, what have you been doing with those fingers then?" Addison chuckles as she squeezes my arm teasingly. Her touch grips me somewhere inside. My face beams red, as I cover it with my hands.

"You Americans are crazy," I don't know what else to say, it's cringe worthy; I hear my words repeat in my head, I hate when that happens.

Addison lands another strike and I realise that she wasn't teasing when she said she'd whip my ass, I thought I was good at bowling, evidently not that good. Anytime she's walking up to take her shot my eyes are glued to her, it must be because I envy her body, it's so perfect, she must work out. Likewise when I'm taking my shots I feel as though she's watching me, maybe she is, of course she is, we're playing a game together, why wouldn't she be.

We haven't stopped laughing and smiling all night, we've talked about so much, just general chat, things like music and movies, conversation that normal people have and not just church life and God. It's like I'm escaping into a secret world, where I can be myself, but am I being myself? Have I really admitted my true feelings to myself, I'm battling with the urge to speak to Addison about my thoughts, I'm scared she will tell Sandra. My parents can never know.

It doesn't take long before it's game over, there was only ever going to be one winner tonight and she's not being humble about it either as she lifts her hands in the air jeering at me. Americans are so loud, well at least this one is but I like it, it's refreshing.

***

Driving home we talk more about Addison's life in New York, how she'd been enjoying studying business studies at college until her Mum took sick and she had to look after her. I feel so sorry for her, being alone over there when that happened. She doesn't mention having any other family and only talks of a few close friends. I learn that she has a brother who practices law in Canada, she doesn't see him often but they talk on the phone. She asks me why I go to church, which I've never been asked before and it's harder to answer than I thought.

"I guess I've always went because of my parents but I love it there and Gregg loves it too." Addison hasn't mentioned having a boyfriend or anything in New York and the nosey side of me wants to ask but I stop myself.

I pull up outside Sandra's house and I don't even want her to get out of the car, I don't know why, there's just something about being in her company that uplifts me, I want to know more about her, I'm intrigued.

"Thanks so much Faith, that was a great night, even if you are a loser, I'll give you a rematch sometime." I shake my head playfully at her as she speaks.

"I'll definitely take you up on that offer and I'll get practicing." I watch and make sure she gets into the house safely and give her a wave and a beep as I drive off, smiling to myself.

CHAPTER 6

I pull the lever on Gregg's slick black leather reclining couch, his house is such a bachelor pad, everything is white and black, he has a huge 52 inch TV on his wall along with photographs of his family that I'm sure his Mum has put up for him.

"Here you go babe," Gregg hands me a warm cup of tea.

"Thank you, I'm exhausted, those classes dragged today Gregg, I can't wait to have all this study behind me." I smile as Gregg sits beside me, giving me a sweet kiss on the cheek.

"I can't wait either, it'll mean more time for us."

More time for us is exactly what we need, deep down somewhere hidden away inside me, I can feel a distance from Gregg, it's not intentional but I just don't feel that we're as close as we once were. Gregg flick on some boring sports channel and I turn my attention to my phone, I never play games on my phone but today during class I was flat out becoming a 10 pin bowling pro. I'll get some more practice in now.

I text Addison to tell her I've been practicing, we've been texting back and forward all day, she's been telling me about her shift in Harmony and about how she's starting to love it over here even though there was a bomb scare in town today, she properly freaked out. That's normal over here though, local people wouldn't see it as a big deal. I got to explain all of that to her today, telling her about our country and the history, she loved it. That makes me smile inside, I'm glad she's happy here, I feel like I'm gaining a close friend and I barely know her.

"Addison is coming for dinner tomorrow night, Mum invited her and Sandra over," Gregg continues looking at the TV as I speak.

"That's good, we should try and get her to church I've heard a few unsavoury rumours about her." There's a hint of disgust in his tone, I'm staring at him, hoping he'll elaborate but he continues watching his sport.

"What have you heard?" I ask, trying not to sound too interested.

"Just that she's a dyke I don't know if it's true, she doesn't really look like one." Gregg's words make my cheeks blush and I try with all my might to keep acting normal but I can't stop myself from defending Addison.

"Lesbians are just people Gregg they don't look a certain way." I retort.

"Aye well most of them look like men, I don't get it, two women together clearly isn't normal like." He shakes his head disapprovingly.

I avoid responding again to Gregg and instead I continue to text Addison, why would he be so nasty, he doesn't even know her. Isn't dyke an offensive word, shouldn't we be showing people love and not animosity? I feel guilty for not standing up for her more but she is living in sin, I guess Gregg just didn't use the best words. No one is perfect, that's what I've learned, not even those in church, though I'd never dare say that out loud. Sometimes it feels like a masquerade, everyone hiding their real faces and showing only what they want others to see. That's what I do, there's so much inside my head I wouldn't dream of saying to anyone, I guess saying it aloud would make it feel more real.

As my mind always does it begins to drift, I think about Addison and how good she looked when we went bowling, I wonder what makeup she uses? Or what products she uses on her hair? I know she works out now, she told me that earlier, though her body gives that away, it's so perfect. Before I know it my mind is drifting away from me, I think about her in a way that I shouldn't. It's not normal to think like this, I just want to be normal. I find myself silently praying that God would tell me why I think like this, why is it that I can't get her off my mind?

The struggle in my mind to battle away the thoughts is one that I'm not winning so far, the prayers aren't helping. I look up at Gregg, moving myself closer to him to kiss his lips softly, it's a welcome distraction for me and Gregg finally stops watching his sport. He lifts me in an instant and moves me onto his knee, my legs to the side; I put hands on his neck, looking into those warm brown eyes and kiss him slowly. He returns the kiss, sliding his hands up my thighs and sending shivers up my spine. It doesn't take long before Gregg becomes more passionate, he kisses me roughly, holding onto my hair at the back of my head, I can feel his erection rise under me.

"I love you Faith," he moans in my ear as he kisses down my neck.
"You too" I whisper, how do I know I love him? I mean, we've been together so long, it feels like routine now, Gregg continues to kiss me as my mind begins to wander yet again. I wonder what Addison will wear to dinner tomorrow night, I'd love to have a look in her wardrobe I bet she has loads of

pretty clothes. Will she want to stay and hang out after? When are we going bowling again? Gregg kisses my lips his hand now dangerously high up my thigh but it isn't his face in my head, it's Addison, she's all I'm thinking about and it's enough to make me pull away from Gregg sharply.

"Sorry babe, it's getting late, I should really get home," I can see the disappointment in his eyes but he doesn't say anything, he acts the perfect gentleman and walks me to my car.

Driving home I feel the weight of the world plant down on my weak shoulders, I've just thought about Addison while kissing Gregg, those soft pink lips on mine, her slender fingers running up my thigh. I feel ashamed of myself, like I need to tell someone, I need to confess, I can't bottle this up.

CHAPTER 7

I'm back in Harmony, of course I am, it's my favourite coffee shop and I've been coming here long before Addison worked here, so it's not as if I'm coming here for her I justify the visit to myself. I sit by the window waiting on my caramel latte, I know she's working today but I haven't seen her yet, she's maybe upstairs sorting stock or out the back cleaning, what does it matter? I have work to do. I setup my laptop and begin typing up what will be my last English assignment, I feel a sense of achievement as I type, though it isn't for me to feel proud, I couldn't have done it without God, I say a silent prayer and thank him for bringing me to where I am today. My phone buzzes on the table; Shannon is texting, wanting to go for a run in the morning she goes through these phases of wanting to keep fit and then being depressed because she hasn't lost the exact number of pounds she hoped for.

"Hey pretty," I feel a soft hand give my shoulder a squeeze, I'm wearing a pink vest top and feeling that skin on mine gives me unfamiliar sensations. I can't even see her yet but that American twang is like no other and just hearing it makes my face light up, I'm sure it's as bright as the Northern Lights.

"Hey, how's it going?" I smile, looking up at her tall slender figure, dressed in black skinny jeans which hug her incredible legs; her black Barista shirt is tucked in showing her flat surfboard like stomach.

"You just can't stay away from me can you?" Addison oozes confidence as she speaks, it's admirable for someone so shy like me. I feel as though she teases me, drawing out my innermost sinful thoughts.

"I came here, long before you." I joke eyes trapped on her slightly open shirt, I wonder if she goes to sun beds, how is her skin so flawless? "I've never came here, not yet anyway." It takes a few seconds for my innocent mind to pick up on her humour and she once again reddens my milky skin, I can't help but laugh, I shouldn't, it's wrong but I can't help it. She doesn't laugh, she keeps face straight and gives me a cheeky grin, with that Addison walks away and begins clearing away some tables.

I can't stop watching her, my assignment has been blown out by her charm, her intriguing ways which draw me to her like a penny to a magnet. Except this penny is putting up a fight, resisting the unseen forcing that are pulling me toward her. There is no harm in looking at another girl right? I mean Shannon talks about girls being pretty all the time and how she likes their clothes and style. It worries me more that I'm drawn to what's on the inside. For now though I enjoy watching her move, she has the most incredible bum, like a peach, she must do squats. I'm never going to get any work done here, every time I start typing I'll hear her voice and want to look up to see who she is speaking to. Everyone she talks to ends up laughing and smiling, she's so outgoing and carefree. She helps the old ladies to their seats and has chats with them while they sip over their hot tea, everyone buys into her. It makes me wish I could be like that but I'd just never have the confidence that she has. I don't stay for too long today, my mind just isn't my own and being here doesn't help at all. I slip out without being noticed.

***

I pull the lever to recline on my Mums fancy brown leather sofa, Gregg lifts his arm and I rest my head on his warm chest. Mum's living room is so cosy with the fire lit, decorated with creams, browns and a touch of mustard, the walls are littered with family photographs and scrolls with Bible verses. It's the one place that to me looks a bit cluttered but I'd never tell my Mum that, she would have the place stripped bare.

"Faith, are you not going to put a bit of effort in for our guests coming over?"

Mum pokes her head around the living room door.

"Yes Mum, I've plenty of time," I sigh, knowing that I had no intentions of not looking my best for Addison coming over; for once she didn't need to tell me.

"Go now Faith, I don't want you keeping us back." I know my Mum has to have her way when she says and I'm not willing for this to go any further, I can see Gregg is getting uncomfortable so I relent and push the recliner back.

The table is laid to its finest, as always when Mum is having guests over. Dad sits at the head of the table, mums place is opposite him; Gregg and I are down one side. I sit hoping Addison sits facing me so we can chat but I get anxious and wonder if anyone will notice that I like talking to her. Will they be able to tell that we clearly text all day every day, will it seem strange to them? I've talked about Addison to my family and Gregg and they're happy that I'm making Sandra's niece feel comfortable, anything to make the family look good I suppose. Though none of them have actually spoken to her before, I hope they like her.

I hear Mum chirping loudly in the hallway, welcoming Sandra and Addison warmly.

"I'm just about to serve dinner, let me take your coats, come on through." I smile at them both as they walk through the doorway though Addison has stolen my eye, she's dressed in her signature black leather jacket which hangs open, underneath a black laced top, which shows her smooth skin around chest. Her black skinny jeans have tears in the legs, and those legs are even more incredible that I've noticed before. Dad never let me wear ripped jeans; he said they were for tramps. She's slightly taller than she normally looks tonight with her short black heeled boots, I like her look, she's quite rock.

Addison takes her place facing me and Sandra doesn't waste time in introducing Addison to the table.
"I know you two are great wee friends Faith, Addison was telling me you're always in Harmony working away." Sandra is a short woman probably about 5FT2 with short cropped black hair. She's slightly overweight and always wears jeans and checkered shirts. Her smile is warm and friendly she's one of those people you know have the warmest hearts.
"Yea Sandra, I see you pop in and out but I always have my head buried in my laptop." I smile widely as Mum begins serving dinner.

Addison and I talk about our bowling experience and I tell everyone how I've been practicing, after a while it feels like it's just us two. I've forgotten all about my family or Gregg and whether or not they'll think we're getting on too well or that I've been thinking about her. We tuck into our main course, Dad turns to Addison having sat long enough without making any conversation not that it's his fault he hasn't got a chance.
"So Addison I'm sure you miss New York?" He enquires dryly.

"Yes, it's a lot different over here but I'm getting used to it, I can see myself staying here for a while." I smile watching her as she speaks, glad that she intends on sticking around, I wonder what she would think if she knew how much I think about her, she'd probably think I'm a creep. "What did you do with yourself over there then?" Sometimes when Dad asks questions it's like an interrogation, he doesn't laugh or joke much, he gets awkward and just speaks, a bit like myself. I'm enjoying finding out about Addison without actually asking, so long may the interrogation continue.

"I was at college, studying business but I dropped out to take care of Mom before she passed." Trust Dad to cause an awkward silence at the table, his face turns a shade of red.

"Yes Marj was telling me about your Mum, I'm sorry to hear that, did you live with her in New York then?" Dad asks awkwardly.

Enough of the questions Dad, he's trying to get off topic, this can only be good.

"I moved out during college, I lived with my girlfriend, then we broke up, Mom got sick and I moved back with Mom."

The silence in the room could be cut with a knife. If Dad's face wasn't red before it resembles a beetroot now. As does everyone else's at the table. The tension is equal to none other. I glance at Sandra the embarrassment is seeping out of her pores.

"Are you planning to study again over here then?" The words are out of my mouth before I even engage my brain. The silence is broken and the awkward begins to fade immediately.

"Yea I've been looking into it but I'm just taking it day by day at the minute." Addison smiles at me, the gratitude for breaking the silence obvious. That smile is so perfect and so infectious.

The rest of the evening passes uneventfully, thank goodness. Gregg and I chat with Dad and Addison is caught up in conversation with Mum and Sandra. Come to think of it, Gregg hasn't really spoken to Addison all evening. The night has passed too quickly and it's time for our guests to leave, I wish Addison could stay and hang out with me but I don't want to make things awkward by asking her, plus Gregg is here. As Sandra and Addison leave, as all church going people do, we all line up to give them a hug. I'm last in line, I hug Sandra and she squeezes me tight. I look at Addison her perfect eyes piercing the innermost parts of me. Those perfect lips, that perfect. It's like everything I seen as being perfect before has been crushed down and made into an incredible woman. As she moves closer I smell her perfume, it consumes me, so sweet but sinful. She wraps her long arms around me, pulling me close to her. I feel her breath on my ear; my legs feel like they may give way, my knees weak. I hold on tight, letting go only when she releases me. My heart is pounding out of my chest.

"I'll see you soon Faith." She smiles almost sympathetically, maybe she feels sorry for me? Why would she? Can she tell I feel the way I do?

Mum and Dad go on to bed after some cleaning up. Gregg and I chill on the sofa again. I'm tired, I know I'll go to bed soon but I don't want Gregg to leave just yet, he brings me comfort. Though I think anyone would bring me comfort, anything to distract me from my own mind really.

"That's disgusting isn't it Faith? I can't stop thinking about it she shouldn't be working in a Christian coffee shop while she's living in sin." My heart sinks.

"That's a ridiculous thing to say Gregg." I retort. "It's not

Faith, she's a lesbian, it's of the devil and your Da said the same to me when they left." I sit forward breathing deeply as Gregg's words cause my breath to quicken.

"I need to sleep Gregg, I can't be bothered with this conversation, it's hardly like you and my Dad are perfect saints." Gregg looks confused as to why I'm getting so defensive, have I blown my cover, what cover? I have nothing to hide. I kiss Greggs cheek and walk swiftly out of the room, Gregg calls my name.

"Just post the key through the door Gregg, I'm exhausted."

I am exhausted but I'm also furious at Gregg for speaking like that and at myself for getting so defensive, I mean it is sin but did she really choose it?

I couldn't stay with Gregg a second longer. I need to be alone, alone with my thoughts and feelings. I lie in bed, my mind running marathons, why did I just get so defensive, isn't what Gregg said true? Though Addison is my friend, I don't want anyone running her down but it doesn't feel like just that. I don't feel like I'm just defending a friend, it's deeper than that. I feel like his words were a personal insult to me, like he's slapped me round the face. It only adds to the increasing gap I feel between me and Gregg. Why am I questioning whether he is right for me, this hasn't happened the whole 6 years we've been together. Is it because I'm so drawn to Addison? What is wrong with me? The confusion is giving me a headache, I just want answers. I turn to the only one I know to turn to when I need answers and begin to pray silently.

CHAPTER 8

Why must Mum Hoover at this time of the morning? I briefly consider getting up to help her but get diverted by a flashback of the time I spent all day cleaning the house for her while she was at the gym. When Dad got home he complained of a 'weird smell' and didn't even notice all of my hard work. It's strange that it was enough to make me cry, it's like sometimes I just want him to thank me or appreciate me. Anything I manage to achieve is never me, it's never my hard work, it's God.

I lie on my back, opening Facebook on my iPhone to have my morning browse which helps me waken, a friend request and a message, I'm popular today. When I click on the request my thumb accepts it within a heartbeat.

You are now friends with Addison Preston. My mind dashes, she added me in the middle of the night, was she thinking about me? I bet the message is from her too. I click on my inbox, Facebook messenger takes a few seconds to load though it feels like a lifetime.

-Hey Faith, I just wanted to say thanks for having us over last night, was great to see you again, thanks for saving me when I dropped the girlfriend bombshell, oops lol I need to beat your ass again at bowling soon. Xx A. Before I even reply I'm scrolling through Addison's profile photos, she looks amazing all of the time, like really. Wow she has photos of her in a bikini on Facebook! If I had a body like hers I'd be posting photos of myself too, well no I wouldn't, my Dad would kill me.

-Hey Addison, awk don't worry at all I'm glad you both came over. Yea I'm sorry about that, my Dad was asking a lot of questions. I'll beat you at bowling some night next week lol I'm going to town for new shoes and coffee today if you want to join me? Xox

-Morning, Yea I don't think he meant any harm with his questions, just opened a can of worms. My Aunt Sandra wasn't too pleased with me anyway, I listened to it the whole way home. Yea I could probably do coffee today then I'm adamant on finding a good pub tonight if you fancy it? Xx A

-Yea I don't think he meant harm either, we just don't agree with it that's all but it's nothing against you, Sandra will come around, she was probably just embarrassed. Yea that would be good, I wouldn't go to a pub, my Dad would freak, sorry Xox

-Probably best I don't get into that, she has nothing to be embarrassed about, I'm me, I'm not going to pretend to be someone I'm not. It's crazy. I guess we'll have to agree to disagree. You guys have nothing to worry about it's not like I'm contagious LOL so what time are you heading to town? P.s I've never met someone your age that doesn't drink, I thought in Ireland everyone loved a drink lol Xx A

-Yea I'd say the rest of the country drink enough to make up for those that don't lol. I can pick you up from Sandra's about 1? Xox -Thanks, That sounds like a plan, I better get a few more hours sleep before then lol, I'll see you soon Faith Xx A

I'm tired but I'll never be able to sleep knowing I'm meeting Addison for coffee. Thinking about seeing her again just stirs up my emotions and my physical senses. I continue scrolling through her profile pictures. She definitely likes a drink and doesn't always wear as much clothes as when I see her. I squeeze my legs together as between my thighs begin to heat up, what is actually wrong with me? My thoughts are warped, I need God to keep me strong, I've heard about how the devil gets inside your mind, making you think disgusting things. I spend the next hour in prayer until my Mum calls me for breakfast.

Bacon eggs and toast, I love when Mum makes my favourite food. Dads off to play Golf today, Mum and I sit at the table and devour our food. "What are you doing today then Faith?" Mum questions as she sips on her coffee.

"I've a few bits to get in town then I'm going to meet Addison for a coffee." The concern on Mums face makes me instantly frustrated. I set me cutlery down and look up from my half eaten breakfast.

"Aren't we supposed to love everyone Mum and not judge people?" I raise an eyebrow, feeling my cheeks blush.

"Yes we are Faith but your Dad isn't going to be happy with this at all. You know bad company corrupts good habits." Mum is genuinely concerned and I can tell that but why can't she just see what I see in Addison.

"Don't be so absurd Mum, you're as bad as Gregg. I'm going to meet Shannon and go for a run." I clear my dishes away in silence.

***

Shannon and I take a much needed breather on a wooden bench in the park close to our homes, it's a massive park with thousands of trees and if you come early enough in the morning you see loads of squirrels running around, I love that. "So tell me about Gavin? When are you seeing him again?" I ask, immediately Shannon's smile is like a Cheshire cat.

"Tonight, I can't wait, that's why I'm running this morning, so my dress fits perfect we're going out for dinner." My smile beams back at my best friend.

"You'll have to send me a snapchat once you're ready. I'm going to meet Addison for a coffee today and getting those new shoes from Office I've been dying to get." I can see the envy on Shannon's face.

"I'm definitely borrowing those shoes, just watch I've heard she's a lesbo, she might try something." With that Shannon stands up and stretches out, I can't bring myself to respond, I can't fight this battle, it's not mine to fight, I've used those words myself so why are they bothering me so much now?

CHAPTER 9

I've just finished getting ready, it's 12:30 in the afternoon, I'm usually never ready on time but I'm as excited as a kid at Christmas, I can't shake the feeling, not that I want to because I haven't felt so good in so long. I've opted to wear something a little dressier than my signature hooded jacket. I've put on a maroon stringy chevron vest top, tucked into black skinny jeans, along with an open denim shirt and matching maroon brogues. My long blonde hair hangs in loose waves and I tuck it behind my ear at one side, smiling to myself in the mirror. I grab my oversized River Island handbag and head off.

I make the short drive over to Sandra's house and park up outside. I'm energized and apprehensive. I just hope I don't act awkward after spending so long staring at her photos on Facebook this morning. I feel I know so much about her that she hasn't told me, the names of her American friends, what her ex-girlfriend looks like, amazing by the way. I sit and think of what we can talk about over coffee. 1:05PM, should I beep? Is that rude? I'll give it another few minutes. 1:08PM, I give a soft push of my horn. Addison is probably taking ages to get ready. I bet that's why she always looks so good. I see Sandra peering out the blinds. This is awkward; I better go to the door.

Sandra meets me at the front door. "Is Addison around?" I smile, the smell of home belts out of Sandra's door, she must be cooking up a storm.
"No dear, a friend came and picked her up about an hour ago,

she said she wouldn't be back until late, is everything alright?"
I try and hide the shock and confusion at her words as I
swallow hard.

"Everything's okay, we were maybe going to grab a coffee but
I'll come by some other time, I'll see you soon Sandra." I smile
widely trying to mask my feelings. "That will be nice for you
two to get together, she said she might come along to church
with me but I doubt it, I'll see you again Faith love." I pay no
notice to Sandra's church comment.

"Thanks Sandra, I'll see you later."

I get in the car slamming the door hard, I'm so annoyed, why
would she not even text me? I don't even want to go to town
anymore, why is this bothering me so much? I mean she could
have let me know. That's just plain rude. I'll get my shoes
another time.

Dad's car is parked up, I don't want to listen to them two go
on at me for meeting Addison, then having to tell them she
stood me up, well she didn't stand me up, it wasn't a date.
Anyway, I creep into the house and head straight upstairs,
crawling into bed and heading for a nosey on Facebook to
distract myself. Maybe she has checked in somewhere, should
I text her? Maybe she forgot or was just running late? No she
would have text and let me know surely. I can't stop thinking
about why she's done this to me, it's like I've been let down
by a life-long friend. I can't get rid of the deep sense of
disappointment; I was looking forward to seeing her so much.
I feel like seeing her takes me away from all of the crazy
thoughts I have, when I'm with her I can just be me. I don't
need to constantly talk about church or my perfect life. I don't
know why it's hurting me so much, if she knew she would
think I was actually mental. I won't tell her, I'll pretend I'm
not bothered. Gregg stood me up before and I don't

remember feeling anything like this, I don't understand.

I hear the sound of my Dad's voice raise, my parents are arguing on the landing. "How many times, I'm the one going out every day to earn the money for you to book a weekend away every other month." Dad gets angry sometimes because Mum doesn't work but how can she work when he expects the house kept perfect and three meals a day laid out for him? "Liam I know you are, the girls from church suggested the weekend away, I couldn't say no." My Mum deserves a break and my Dad should know that.

"Well maybe their husbands are stupid enough to hand their bank cards over but I'm not." Dad's voice is becoming louder, it sounds like he's almost spewing venom.

"I would make my own money Liam but you told me I shouldn't work, I look after the house and run after you all day." I hear a loud smack and my Mum's screams rip through my ear drums and shatter my soul.

"You wouldn't have anything if it wasn't for me you stupid bitch." Dad scowls. My Mum's bedroom door slams hard and I can hear her sobs next door as Dad thumps down the stairs. In this house he is the head, she shouldn't speak back to him, I heard him quote a scripture about wives submitting to their husbands before.

I know better than to get involved. My Mum will only tell me that it is her fault and that my Dad has done nothing wrong. The last time he hit her I was in the next room and when I asked her about it she said I must have imagined it. I bury my head deep under my duvet, hiding away from my perfect life. My tears have soaked my pillow, I don't want this to be real but it is. It has been real from as far back as I remember. Being a little girl maybe 7 or 8 and cowering in my closet as my Dad beat my Mum so bad she couldn't leave the house for weeks. Why does he do it? At church he's the perfect husband, the perfect Dad, the perfect man, why doesn't my Mum leave him?

My phone buzzes in my hand, Gregg is calling I let it go to voicemail, not now Gregg. I've never told him about my Dad before and I'm not about to either. He thinks my Dad is amazing because he has a business and makes money, giving a lot of it to the church. That doesn't make him a perfect person. He's far from it though he wears his Christian mask well at church. I continue to sob as my Mum's scream repeat in my head again and again.

CHAPTER 10

Crying until I drift off to sleep is normally something I reserve for the evenings but this afternoon nap is an exception. I wake up on top of my bed clothes feeling heavy headed and groggy. I try and force aside the sound of my Mother's scream, I know too well that if I go downstairs her and my Dad are probably cuddled up on the sofa watching the God channel acting like nothing ever happened. Then there's Addison, what a bitch. I need to deal with Gregg too, I've barely been speaking to him, I feel like my insides are pushing him away and I can't stop it, I don't even want to see him.

I lift my phone, 5pm, I feel like I've been asleep for 10 minutes, not hours, I must have needed that. I haven't been sleeping great for months now. I spend most nights lying praying for hours to stop my mind from wandering off into the perversion that the devil lays out for me on a plate for me. I check Facebook then notice I have some private messages, it's Addison, how did I not see these earlier?
12:25 PM -Hey Pretty, sorry for letting you down so late, I forgot I'd told a friend I'd meet her for a drink today, I'll see you next week for some bowling Xx A

3:30 PM -Sandra said you stopped by, you mustn't have got my message, I'm really sorry, I'll make it up to you, I promise. Xx A. How embarrassing, she knows I went to pick her up and probably thinks I'm a sad act. I sigh loudly. I don't know why I even care or why she is so inside my head. Who is her friend? Is it a date?

-Hey Addison, awk don't worry, I didn't head into town anyway. We'll catch up another time, have fun Xox

Now I need to deal with Gregg, though at least I won't have to see him tonight, he's away out with his friends to the cinema, maybe I want to see him, I need comfort. Sometimes I feel like I want to be close to him, other times his very voice is enough irritate me for hours, I try not to dwell on the negative thoughts and instead force them to the black hole in my brain. We've been together forever and everyone says we're meant to be, he's the perfect man.

-Hey babe, sorry I haven't been in contact much, I've had so much work to do and haven't been feeling great, I'll see you at church in the morning? X

I'll catch up on some TV. It'll give me a distraction from what is becoming a very miserable existence inside my own mind. To others I smile and laugh, have my assignments done on time and go to church every week but to me I'm trapped living with a sinful secret that repulses me to the core. I'll slip into someone else's reality for a while and avoid my own. I haven't watched the apprentice this year, it's on episode 7, that'll do for a good few hours entertainment.

Gregg eventually texts back at 11pm and I finally take my eyes of the Apprentice before Lord Sugar's face becomes etched into my brain, not that I watch the show for him, I watch it for Karren Brady as I've always loved her from as far back as I remember, she's a role model and incredibly gorgeous.

-Hey gorgeous, no sweat, I've been busy myself, had a great night out there with the lads, I'll take you out for a wee date this week. I'll see you in the morning bright and early xx

1:00AM has come so fast, I yawn as I switch the TV off, that apprentice marathon was exactly what I needed. Now a creep on Facebook and I'll be out like a light, it's like the past day never happened. I scroll through boring status updates, watching the odd makeup tutorial, I always wonder how long it takes to sit and edit those, all for a few likes.

Addison Preston 20 mins ago -Belfast centre nightmare for gettin cab, take me back to NYC.

I breathe deeply, is she okay? Why is she in the city Centre at this time of the morning? How will she get home? She must be drunk given the typo.

-Hey Addison, did you get a taxi? Xox

-Nooo nightmare Xx

-Are you alone? Where are you? Xox -Yea, the gay bar, Kremlin Xx

-I can come and take you home? Xox

-No don't be silly, I'll get a cab it's late Xx

-No I will, it's dangerous, you don't even know this place, I'll leave now and call you when I'm outside. Xox

-Thanks so much Faith Xxxx

I jump out of bed pulling my jeans and a jacket on and scrape my hair back into a messy bun. I don't have time to fix my face or make sure I look okay, a quick dab of rose coloured lipstick will do. I pull on my Ugg boots and creep out into the landing, almost silently walking downstairs. My parents will be out like lights at this time. I've never sneaked out before. It gives me a little thrill knowing I'm doing something they don't know about. Normally they know every detail of my existence.

The whole journey is plagued with worried thoughts about Addison, I just want to know she's safe, how could she be so careless as to leave herself stuck with no way home, she doesn't even know this place. I've forgotten all about her standing me up as I pull up outside the Kremlin. I know exactly where this place is because every year at the Gay pride march they hold an outdoor event and our church holds a protest on the opposite side of the road. I've stood here many a time telling people like Addison that they're heading straight for hell. The streets are littered with drunken people, singing and eating take away. It looks quite fun compared to how they describe clubbing in church. I call Addison.

"I'm outside the front..."

"Okay give me 2 mins Thanks Faith bye.... Yea I'll take 1" What's she taking? That's strange.

Addison opens the car door, the smell of drink overpowering, she throws her cigarette down and crushes it with her black stiletto heel before almost falling into the car and closing the door, she turns to me her face beaming and I can tell she's drunk. Being drunk doesn't stop her looking like some sort of a Goddess, those long legs. She must be feeling the heat in her little black dress and stilettos, her leather jacket doesn't look like it's giving her much warmth. I can't take my eyes of that pearly white smile. She reaches in her bag pulling out a white plastic rose and giggles sweetly.

"This is for picking me up, I wanted pink but she only had white." I blush and laugh awkwardly. "Awk you shouldn't have, thank you. I've heard about the rose sellers but I've never been given one of their roses." I take the rose and place it down the side of my car door as we share a laugh together. I've only been in her company a few minutes and already she has unknowingly lifted a weight off my shoulders.

"Did you have a good night then?" I ask glancing over as often as I can whilst driving.

"Yea, People over here are so friendly and the music was

great, I'm sorry I couldn't make it earlier, but I'll treat you to a Mcflurry now?" She points to the big M sign in front of us.

"Sure I guess that'll do." I smile, trying to keep my eyes of those amazing pins of hers. I just want to run my hand along her thigh, see if they are as smooth as they look. Why am I even thinking about touching her?

I get ice cream and Addison treats herself to some chips, or as she says 'fries'. I park up in the dark car park, putting the interior light of the car on, her eyes sparkle in the light, pupils enlarged as they burn through my body and cause a heat to rise once again between my thighs. Only she gives me this feeling. I keep looking down, if our eyes meet, will she see the glint in my eye that says I like her more than I should? Will she be able to tell that I can't stop thinking about her every minute of every day and that she's making me question everything I've ever known?

I need to speak before my mind runs away. "You really should be more careful you know arrange a lift home before you go out..." I say softly, showing genuine concern.

"Yea I know, I was supposed to go stay with a friend but she got pissed and started arguing with me and left." Addison doesn't seem too bothered about this as she places a chip between her lips. I feel like I'm staring at the chip, but it's her lips, they look so, kissable.

"You want share?" Addison offers, clearly she thinks I'm glaring at the chip too.

"No I'm okay." I laugh knowing why she offered.

"Is everything okay now, I didn't realise you had friends over here yet?" I'm being nosey and I don't care, I want to know who she was with, if it was a date?

"Well I guess she's not a friend, more a potential fuck buddy, she's married I met her online." Addison laughs and even though I don't find it funny, I can't help but smile when she does, I am in shock though, a married woman? Having sex with Addison? She's obviously married to a man, gay marriage is illegal here, I know because we celebrated it staying that way in church. Why would Addison give her body away like that? She deserves so much more. She's worth so much more.

"That's crazy Addison, just be careful." I don't know what else to say, I don't want to judge her, though I already am in my head, it's built in now from all these years of Bible Bashing others.

"I always am, you're such a sweet girl Faith, you're not like the rest of those Church ones, I can tell."

How can she tell that I'm different? Is my mask falling off, I've been trying so hard for years to be the same as them and now she's telling me I'm not. I think she thinks it's a compliment but it's not, it hurts to know I'm not normal like them.

"I do think the same about sin and stuff. I just try not to judge people based on that. People in church aren't always as perfect as they make themselves out to be," I look down at my hands on my lap, what am I saying, I'm running Christians down, this isn't me.

"Yea they are, come on, like your Mom and Dad have the perfect little home, cars, job, daughter, the only thing you're all missing is a halo," Addison's tone has changed, she sounds more emotional, I've not really seen this side to her, I've just seen happy go lucky Addison with not a care in the world.

As she talks about my perfect family I feel myself thrown back to the sound of the loud smack across my Mums face earlier. "That's not true Addison, everyone has imperfections," except you.

"Yea, yea, you have the perfect life and it's nothing to be ashamed of." Addison is trying to play around but I'm not feeling it, she shouldn't think I have the perfect life, I don't. I hate myself; I spend every night crying as I wallow in self-loathing.

"You have no clue what you're talking about, I might seem happy and my family might seem happy but I'm not and neither of they, so don't judge me, I haven't judged you," my tone is serious. I've never spoken to her like that before and I'm anxious as to how she'll react, I want to retract my words, what if she asks me questions?

"Shit Faith, I didn't mean to piss you off, what's wrong." The anger is fading and I feel myself becoming emotional, seriously Faith, pull it together.

"It's nothing, just forget I said anything." I feel a tear escape from my eye and roll down my cheek, what am I becoming? I can't get through a few hours without becoming an emotional wreck.

Addison reaches over putting her soft slender hand on mine, making my insides flip.

"Is there something you want to talk about Faith? You can talk to me and trust me." I contemplate pouring out my secrets to Addison but I can't, I'm so full of fear, I've held them in for so long, I've never wanted to tell, why do I want to now? Would she even care?

"No, I don't want to talk," more tears begin to stream down my face now as my cheeks blush, I'm so embarrassed, she's going to think I'm a freak.

"Awk no, come here." Addison pulls me close, holding me tight, the smell of her perfume, her touch, why does this girl make me feel so alive. I hold her not letting go, sobbing into her shoulder, as she gently rubs my back.

"It's going to be okay girl..." I put my arms around her and don't let until all of my tears are cried, she plants a small kiss on the top of my head.

"I'm here, anytime you need, you hear me?" She moves back looking into my eyes, I look down unable to stand the feelings she makes me feel. "Thank you, I'm sorry for being a mess." Jokingly she looks me up and down, then stares intently into my eyes which have wandered back to hers.

"You're a lot of things Faith but a mess is definitely not one of them."

Was that a compliment, it was, is she saying I look good, maybe she likes my jacket, there's no way she's talking about my appearance in general. I'm glad we've gotten past my train wreck moment there, we've finished our food long ago and it's getting really late, I start the car up and begin to drive. Addison is back to herself again, carefree, singing along to Mumford and Sons.

"So Faith, when are you coming to stalk me in Harmony again, I bet you've missed me?" she can barely hold in her giggle as she says it, when she's drunk it must be harder to keep the mysterious tone and straight face she normally has when making comments like that. Flirting, is that what she's doing? Maybe I should play this game back and just ask her, I can feel my cheeks becoming flushed before I even say it but she's drunk and that gives me confidence for whatever reason. "Are you flirting with me Addison?" Her loud laugh almost startles me.

"Do you want me to be flirting with you?" I'm crawling back into my hole, my moment of confidence is knocked and she has the upper hand, I should have seen that coming. I let out a loud sigh shaking my head jokingly, I know she's watching me and I know she knows she's won.

I pull up outside Sandra's house.

"Drink some water before you sleep, I've heard that helps a hangover." I take another peek at Addison's legs as she undoes her seat belt. "Nothing helps... Aunt Sandra is going to try and make me go to church too but I wouldn't want to spread my disease," I look up at her eyes confused.

"What disease?" She laughs at me.

"You know my lesbianism, unless you want to catch it," Addison is being more forward tonight than she's ever been, she's staring me straight in the eye and her look is no longer menacing, it's heated, like at any minute she could rip my clothes off, am I imagining this? It's just that charm, it doesn't matter what she's saying, I'm just pulled in.

"Wise up you, give me another one of your lesbian hugs." I joke as she wraps her arms around me, these are the best hugs, I don't want her to stop, I don't want her out of the car, I hold onto her tightly, breathing her in.

"You know, joking aside Faith, you can talk to me anytime you need, I'm here, you've been a good friend to me," the warmth of her breath on my ears spreads between my legs like wildfire. My mind is playing tricks on me, telling me to touch her leg, to kiss her, disgusting things, stop. I pull myself away. "Goodnight."

CHAPTER 11

This is not how I intended on starting my Sunday morning however it's happening and I can't stop it, I need it. Those eyes, that skin, the smile, the laugh, everything about her, makes me want her, need her. I want to be close to her, I don't want anyone or anything else, what is wrong with me, why can't I stop this? I push the guilty feelings aside, I can't have it ruining this moment for me, the moment I've been waiting for, for so long.

Addison and I are sporting skimpy pyjama shorts and stringy tops. She lies on her side in the bed beside me.

"Take your clothes off," her command is dry and serious, I wouldn't dare to disobey. I slide my shorts off and pull my top over my head, I feel exposed, I've never been naked with someone else before, the look she gives my body gives me shivers, there are almost hearts in her eyes as she slowly draws her attention back up to mine.

"Do you want me to take my clothes off Faith? Would you like that?" I nod slowly, not wanting to look too eager, I need to see her body I know it's perfect.

Addison pulls her clothes off and stays lying beside me, her curvy figure makes my heart thump, her skin is just as flawless as I imagined. I turn my focus to her nipples; they're hard and dark, sitting so delicious on her pert breasts. "Why don't you touch them Faith?" Her words distract me. I look back up to her eyes. "What?" I feel my breath getting heavier. "Why don't you touch them Faith? You're looking at them, you

must want to touch them," she slides her hand on top of my hand and leads
it to her hard nipple, squeezing my hand to make me caress her silky soft breast.
"Do you like that?" I swallow hard, nodding. "Yes." I say quietly as I feel my cheeks becoming redder.

"What's wrong Faith? You don't have to be embarrassed. You have an amazing body, you want me to touch it don't you?" As if in a trance I nod my head, every word she speaks through those perfect pink lips is like a drug to me, setting my insides on fire and causing moisture between my thighs.
"Why don't you touch yourself first?" With one movement, Addison has taken my other hand and is sliding it slowly down my stomach to my pelvic bone.
"Touch yourself how you want me to touch you," She slides my hand over my smooth slit, the heat rising and hitting my fingers instantly, teasing me, she moves my hand back and forward slowly, before pressing down on my fingers putting pressure on my clit. I let out a soft moan, her eyes burning on mine.
"You like that baby?" She knows I like it, my body is jolting under our touch. My toes curl into my bed sheets.

Addison leans down kissing my lips softly, as she puts more pressure on my fingers, forcing them to move in circular motions; my body is hers now I've given it up to her. I can't control it anymore, what is this feeling? What is she doing to me? She stops kissing me looking directly into my eyes.
"Come for me Faith." Like a command I...

"Faith, sweetie, time to get up please," I hear my Mum's voice from the hallway and freeze still like a deer in headlights, removing my hand from between my legs. I've snapped back to reality, I've just came, I've never touched myself like that before, I can barely breathe to answer my Mum back, I don't want her coming in here. "Okay," I call back, trying to hide my panting breaths. I don't know how that happened, I started looking at photos of Addison on Facebook and the heat between my legs came back, next thing my eyes were shut and I was fantasising while touching myself. I feel so dirty, like it's really happened, like I'm a lesbian, a sinner, this is so wrong. I don't have any other words, just wrong but it felt so right, even in my head. I finally manage to control my breathing and pick myself up to get ready for church. I head straight for the shower. I can't shake the feeling of repulsion off. The puddle between my legs only reminds me of how ashamed I should be of myself for allowing those thoughts to manifest so much that I've just done that, whatever that was.

***

I sit in church with my Mum and Dad at one side and Gregg on the other, Pastor Leacher begins his Sunday morning service, everyone seems so happy to be here, everyone except me. From the moment I stepped through the door, I feel like everyone is watching me, like they know what I've done this morning, they know how disgusting I am and that I don't belong here. I couldn't even look Gregg in the eye when I first saw him, I feel like I've betrayed him, like I've been with someone else, Addison of all people, I have been, in my mind, unfaithful.

The only thing I've paid attention to this whole service is the amount of times the Pastor refers to homosexuality, three times. Once to condemn the ongoing campaign for same-sex marriage, once along with the words rape and murder and finally to link it to the increasing suicide rate of young people in our country. Doesn't the church have a responsibility to then reach out to those people rather than condemn them? Surely being likened to a rapist or a murderer isn't going to discourage a young gay person from ending their life. Do I really believe all of this? It's all I know. Is this the devil trying to pull me into a perverted mind set, beginning with empathy for those living in sin?

CHAPTER 12

Mummy makes the best Sunday dinners and today is no exception, I've eaten so much roast chicken I could bust at the seams. I try and relax in my room, contemplating the past few days and the overwhelming sense of guilt that I can't shake. I go through phases of wanting to write down my thoughts, though I'd never dare to write down what I wouldn't want anyone else to see. Even writing something down that isn't right in God's eyes would seem like a sin to me. I've found an old diary and am reminiscing about how I used to be, long before the horrible thoughts began, when I felt like a strong young woman of God. How do I get back to that place?

What's the point in this life, to face heartache pain and strife?
Or to live to the full, enjoying every day? Perhaps go along a narrow set out way?
People have discussed this life, various opinions have arose,
Some think there's no point and if there is, nobody knows.
So ask yourself what's the point in your living? To be a good person and always be giving

Or are you here because we evolved millions of years ago?
Maybe a huge explosion blew up nothing, causing us to grow?
Perhaps you have a creator, who looks over you from above,
Who wants to protect you and surround you with love?
Sadly, the only thing you're guaranteed is to die, So what's the point, please ask yourself why. It's hard not to question if there's something round the bend,
Is there more to life, or is death the end?

I believe there's more, though it's hard for us to tell.
I believe in an all-powerful God, an afterlife, I believe in heaven and hell.
I believe in all we do we should always do our best,
We shouldn't compete to be better than the rest. I believe God sent his one and only son,
When we die, we'll face him and have nowhere to run.
So that's what life's all about?
Living for God? I believe it, without a doubt. Eternity is real; it can't be ignored or put to the side,

Heaven is where you'll spend it, if God is your guide.
If you let Satan deceive you, or faith is what you lack,
You're eternity will be spent in hell and there's no turning back!

Reading over those words gives me a burning sensation in my chest, as if I'm pining for a once strong Faith. Lately I'm finding church hard, I hate thinking about it, I always try and force the thoughts away by praying, reading the Bible or listening to some Christian music but it's time I face up to the fact that I am questioning my faith and myself. Is it the devil getting inside my head? making me feel like I'm different? Or is it that I am different and I can't change that? I don't know. Who can help me? Who can I turn to? I would never be accepted for the person I might be behind this Christian mask, the fear of rejection makes me weep softly.

When I need comfort or a shoulder, Gregg and Shannon are my go to people but I feel such a distance between us, like I'm hiding something from them. I've never felt like this before, normally the height of my worries are my studies or my relationship with God. I can't bear to turn to them, how can I tell Gregg that when we sit down to watch Eastenders the only thing I care about is getting to see Samantha Womack? Or tell Shannon that when we talk about loving David Beckham, the only thing I love about him are his football skills and not the looks Shannon goes on about? I'd much rather look at his wife. How can I tell them that Addison has become my obsession? They'll think I'm a freak. I am a freak.

I need to let this out. I can't hold it in any longer, I need someone to hear, to listen, to understand, the weight of my dirty secret is tearing my life apart. Shattering everything I once dreamed of. I hold my phone to my ear, each ring feels like a lifetime, my heart beats like one of those bass drums the bands play at the 12th parades. "Hello." I'm silent; I can't even get a word out. This is a mistake. I should just hang up. "Faith?"

"Hey, it's me, sorry." My voice is shaking. "Are you okay? What's the matter?"

"I'm okay, I just wanted to talk." "Okay, well I'm here to listen."

"Please don't say anything Addison, you promise?" I swallow hard, trying to stop tears from flowing.

"I promise. You're worrying me, should I come over?"

"No, I'm okay I just need to let this out, I can't hold it in for another second, I hate myself so much."

"Faith, you don't sound okay, do you want to come here? Why are you saying you hate yourself?"

"No, no it's okay. I just can't stop these thoughts, I know they're wrong, well I believe they're wrong, I'm scared of offending you but I don't know who else to talk to."

"You won't offend me sweetie, I'm tough. Keep talking." Addison's voice is soft and genuine. I wish she was here to hold me.

"I don't even know how to say it, what's going on in my mind, the thoughts, I've had them for so many years but I've buried them, now they won't go away, I can't sleep, I can't function."

"Faith, just breathe. Tell me, what are the thoughts?" I can hear the concern in Addison's voice, finally, someone who cares about me and not just what God thinks of me.

"I can't say it. It's wrong, it's perverted. If a couple walk down the street, I look at the girl, why?"

The line is silent for a few seconds, does Addison think I'm a freak too. Saying the words make the tears stream down my hot cheeks.

"Okay Faith, those feelings are normal for some people. You know, not every girl wants to look at a man, I know I don't. Your church tells you these things are wrong, that doesn't make it true. There's nothing wrong with how you feel."

"I can't deal with it Addison, I don't want to feel this, I don't want to look at girls."

"It's not a choice Sweetie, people are born differently, I didn't choose to like girls. It's not something we can control."

"I need to control it, God says its sin, I have a boyfriend, I love him. My family will hate me." "Why don't you come over Faith? We can talk more, I don't want you alone when you're upset."

"I can't, I have to go to church soon. I'm too ashamed to say it to anyone's face." "Please don't feel like that Faith, you have nothing to be ashamed of, why don't I come to church with you and we can talk after? You know that would make Sandra's Sunday."

I smile, giggling a little, I know how pleased Sandra would be, I love that Addison is offering to come to church with me, maybe I won't feel so alone even though I'm surrounded by people. "I would love that. Can I pick you up at 6? I need to get ready now."

"Okay honey, I'll brush my hair and make myself a little more presentable, shall I?"

"I'm sure you look just fine, I'll see you soon and thank you, just please don't say."

"You can trust me Faith. Don't forget that. See you shortly."

CHAPTER 13

I sit in the car outside Sandra's house, texting Addison to tell her I'm outside. I feel those butterflies in my stomach that only she gives me. I'm like a bag of nerves. I can't believe I've told her my secret. I can't believe I've said it out loud. What has happened to me, my whole world is falling apart, my perfect world I've been building for years. Anxiety begins to ripple through my whole being, like a huge splash in a tiny pond, it makes me nauseous. I'm on the verge of driving off when Addison pulls open the car door.

I can only assume the colour has drained from my face, usually when I see Addison my cheeks flush, she probably thought until now my skin was pink. I stare straight ahead, I can't even look at her, after what I done this morning, what I told her on the phone, why am I even with her? Her perfume fills my lungs. It's comforting somehow, but why?
"Faith you look real pale honey." Addison's hand rests on my shoulder.
"Are you sure you're okay to drive?" Her voice soothes me, like a dummy for a screeching child, every word taking away a piece of my anxiety.

"I don't know, I don't know if I'm okay, I don't know anything."

"Aunt Sandra's gone to church, why don't you park round back and come inside, church isn't for another 30 minutes?" I don't want to go to church, I never feel like this, I always want to be there, it isn't giving me what I need, being there isn't helping me anymore. Am I past saving? "Okay, I can't have anyone seeing my car," I drive round the back of the house and park out of sight. Pulling my seatbelt off, like I'm freeing myself, if only really being free was so easy. There's an atmosphere in the car and I'm creating it, Addison has asked me to talk but I can't, I haven't even looked at her yet.

"I need air." I jump out of the car and stand breathing the cold air in deeply my head in my hands.

I feel Addison wrapping her arms around me tightly, sending that familiar rush through my body even in my current state she still has that effect. I bury my head in her chest, soaking her top with my tears.

"I'm so confused." I sob more, my body convulsing as she rubs my back softly.

"Let's get you inside. It's Baltic as you would say." Her joke brings a small glimpse of a smile to my face, only she could manage that. Why is it only her? Why can't Gregg make me feel so alive even when parts of me feel so dead?

Addison walks me in and sits me down on Sandra's beige fabric sofa.

"Can I get you something to drink?" I finally look up at Addison who is standing a few feet in front of me. She looks down, smiling empathetically. Can she empathise? Has she felt how I felt? Her leather jacket has been replaced by a long black dress coat with a smart grey top, she looks smarter than usual maybe she put on her Sunday best. Her black jeans still visible but she's opted for the ones without the rips and a smart pair of grey brogues. Her outfit is distracting me a little, which can only be a good thing.

"I'm okay, thanks." I try and force a smile, wiping the tears off my face.

I can feel her eyes burning on me as I sit staring straight ahead, I don't know what to say, I can't explain how I feel because I don't know how I feel. She's letting the silence force me to speak, I can't stand the silence.

"Addison, I just don't know what's going on in my head. Am I gay?" The words spit out of my mouth quickly, making me sob again, it's the first time I've said it so bluntly out loud and the fear sweeps through my body like an angry flame. Addison places her arm around my shoulder holding me as I cry uncontrollably.

"I wish I could answer that for you Faith, only you know how you feel honey, all I know is no matter what, I'll be here for you, you don't have to go through this alone."

I don't know how long I've been crying for. Addison is still cradling me like a pathetic emotional wreck. I'm definitely not making church, I know I've been here for that long. I wipe my face again, holding my head in my hands and trying to gather myself, I need to think straight.

"I should text my parents and Gregg to tell them I'm not coming, what can I say?" I look at Addison and she shakes her head unsure.

"I don't know Faith, why don't you tell them you aren't feeling so well?" I send the messages and set my phone aside, turning to look at Addison, I know my face is red and puffy but I'm past caring, my eyes meet hers and I feel a bit of colour return to my face like my blood has suddenly remembered to flow. I breathe deeply, I feel like I'm about to deliver a speech in the style of Martin Luther King Jnr.

"I had a dream Addison that I would grow up to marry

Gregg, he would be the perfect husband and we would have the perfect family. I would be the perfect Christian wife and Mother, nothing could ever go wrong." I gasp for air and breathe out slowly, swallowing to remove the lump from my throat. Addison nods to tell me she's listening, she probably doesn't want to interrupt or say anything in case I turn into an emotional mute again.

"For years I've played along to this, the Christian way of life, it's all I know. I noticed when I was a teenager I'd grow attached to certain people, like a particular teacher, she was so lovely and she looked amazing, I would think about her, more than I should, I never told anyone this, I just hid it away, thinking it was because maybe I wanted to be like her when I was older." I take another huge breath.

"Okay, Sweetie." Addison reaches over and takes my hand, caressing it, her physical touch a massive comfort.

"I noticed this more as time went on, maybe a woman on TV, Karren Brady, I love her, everything about her, the way she looks everything, I never thought of anything sexual really, but then I wouldn't it's not how my brain is trained. When I'm intimate with Gregg, not that we've had sex but just being close, it doesn't feel right, I want to push him off me and scream." With that my tears stream again and there's no holding them back.

I look longingly into Addison's understanding eyes, watching her lips as she begins to speak. "When I was a teenager, I loved my teacher too, though my brain wasn't trained to not think about sex, I knew I found her sexually attractive, I never felt that with any man and the thought of having a man close to me, well let's just say I never gave it a thought, I just knew all along. My Mum was fine with it, so it was easy for me to question it, I didn't have to hide and even if you are just questioning it, you shouldn't have to keep it bottled up." Hearing that Addison felt something similar to me, that someone understands I'm not just crazy lifts my soul a little.

"You can't force yourself to be with a man and never be your true self because that's what your church says, there are so many churches that accept being gay as being normal, which it is, there is in the US anyway, I don't know about here."

I know there are churches that accept people for being gay because Pastor Leacher has run them into the ground plenty of times. Watered down worldly religion is what he called it.

"I can't tell anyone Addison, it isn't just my church, it's my family, Shannon, Gregg, it would destroy them they would never accept me." My tears are stopping though I think it's more that I have none left to cry rather than me feeling any better.

"I hate myself, I feel repulsed that I think like this, it's the devil, isn't it? I'm going to hell." My voice trembles and panic begins to set in, my mind spinning like a hamster on a wheel. My insides are screaming out for freedom.

"Stop that Faith, stop it. I can't listen to you saying that, it's bullshit, they've washed your brain, you are an awesome girl in fact you're one of the most amazing girls I've ever met." Addison pulls me close to her, I rest my head on her shoulder, I can feel her breath is rapid, this is stirring her emotions up. Those compliments, the kind words she says about me bring me a huge comfort, right now, in her arms, though I remain silent, I feel like a weight is being lifted from me, like my eyes are opening to the fact that maybe I am brainwashed. Maybe they are wrong and being gay is normal and it's not vile and dirty?

***

Addison still has me in her arms and I don't ever want to leave, she rubs my temple gently with her thumb, I've kept my head buried under her arm leaning on her chest. We've talked about how dangerous she feels organised religion is and about how I can still have faith without belonging to or conforming to the beliefs of a church. It's not something I've ever thought about or spoken about before but she makes sense, everything she says makes sense. For once I feel like I'm speaking openly, like someone knows who I am when my mask falls off and more than that someone accepts me without my mask. I've told her I don't think my family would ever accept me if I told them I was gay, and how it would shatter Gregg's heart. By now we're speaking as though I am gay, like its common knowledge. That scares me. Although she tells me I'm only hurting Gregg more by staying, it doesn't seem as easy as that in my head. I do agree though that I should speak to him about how I feel, I just don't know how I would ever do it?

"I don't want to go, but I have to, church will be finishing soon and I need to be home for my parents getting back." I look up into Addison's weary blue eyes. I think I've drained every ounce of energy from her, though she still manages a sweet smile.

"Promise me Faith, you won't allow yourself to feel guilty inside for who you are." I look down again.

"I hope so, I hope I can feel that way," Addison squeezes me one last time and I embrace it, closing my eyes and escaping into our own little world momentarily.

We stand at the back door, Addison places her hands in mine and stands facing me, looking down into my tired puffy eyes.

"I want you to know, you're beautiful, you're amazing, you're perfect exactly how you are and you should be proud of that." I blush, unable to stop a smile from creeping onto my face. I look at the floor nervously, inadvertently squeezing on her soft slender hands.

"Thank you for everything, tonight has meant the world to me, please don't tell anyone." I look up again, wanting to access her face to ensure my secret is safe.

"I promise Faith, you have my word." I'm locked in an embrace with her, my arms wrapped tightly around her body, she kisses the top of my head gently, I don't want to leave but I have to.

It's easier for me to tell Addison how much I appreciate her in a text message. I'm too embarrassed to speak too much to her face. I can lie in bed feeling a million times lighter like I've been on Slimming World and miraculously lost a tonne of weight. I feel I could sleep tonight without any tears. The light on my phone is the only thing keeping me awake, I am exhausted.

-Hi Addison, thank you for everything tonight. You made me feel safe, like finally someone understood and cared about me, not just 'who God wants me to be.' I can't tell you enough how much it means, you're an incredible person. Xoxo

CHAPTER 14

Normally in the morning it takes a while for my brain to begin to function, especially on a Monday, not today though, I wake from my sleep as if someone has beaten a drum in my ear, jolting upright on my bed. What happened last night, the things I said, how I felt, what Addison said, it spins in my head like one of those waltzers at the fairground. It doesn't seem real. It is real though, it happened I know that by the text on my phone from Addison.

-Hey girl, you know I would never tell anyone, I'm always here for you. I'd love to spend more time with you, make sure you're okay give me a call tomorrow xx A

What have I done? I can't actually do this? I can't just accept that I'm that person. That despicable person that my parents will find so grotesque they'll ask me to leave their home. What am I supposed to do? Now that I'm alone without Addison and her comfort it's like I'm back in the trap, caught between God and Gay with no means of escape, no way out that won't ruin my perfect dreams.

"Faith, are you awake?" Mum walks through the door, I try and hide my panicking expression.

"I'm up Mum I have class this afternoon." I smile.

"Are you feeling better? What happened last night?" Mum asks concerned as she leans on my door frame.

"I don't know, it was just my stomach, I'm okay." Mum nods, believing me, I feel terrible for lying but that terrible doesn't even come close to the other emotions I feel.

"Why don't you come down I'll make us some breakfast? Your Dad's off today." Great, I'll have to listen to Dad yap about me not going to church.

"Okay, I'm going to get a shower, I'll be down soon."

I sit at the breakfast table, picking over the full fry my Mum has cooked up, I don't feel like eating at all but I don't want to be ungrateful. Dad's already asked me about why I missed church, when I told him he didn't even ask if I felt better, hmmm, priorities? Except I can't be annoyed because I wasn't even sick to begin with, though my stomach is in knots right now, maybe I am sick.

"Sandra said you were going to bring her niece to church? That's a shame you were sick," Mum forces conversation as me or Dad aren't making any attempt. There's uneasiness at the table, maybe they've had another row.

"Yea, she was going to come but I'll bring her another time."

I take a sip of my hot tea, I used to believe tea fixed everything though I find myself doubting the power of tea right now.

"That girl would need to sort herself out, I've told Pastor Leacher she shouldn't be working in that coffee shop it's disgusting." I almost choke on my tea, it's like Dad knows and he's trying to infuriate me. His eyes watch my reaction, am I being paranoid?

"Dad, gay people should be allowed to work too surely?" My Dad's face tells me that he's unhappy with my response or that I've even dared answer him back, my Mum looks at me disapprovingly.

"It's not about working, it's about working in a Christian run business." I shake my head, setting my cutlery down; I can't force another bite into me.

"You know maybe Sandra needs to be harder on her, giving her a job and a home, I wouldn't have that living under my roof I'd rather you told me you'd terminal cancer than were gay, then at least you could be healed." Those words have just torn straight through every layer of my skin and pierced my heart with such force that I gasp. I can't even force any words out. I don't know what I could say to that, does he know?

"I'm going to the library before class, thanks for breakfast Mum." I walk out of the house, almost in a daze or a state of shock. What just happened?

***

I couldn't tell you a single word that was mentioned in class today. I've never been so disengaged. Those words 'I'd rather you had terminal cancer' are smashing through my brain cells every few minutes. Stirring up rage, hurt and every other emotion designed to test us as human beings. How could I do this to my family? They don't deserve the shame that having a gay daughter would bring to them? What would people think about Gregg, what would they say to him? Would he ever trust anyone again? The Bible study draws to a close and I don't feel like I've heard a single scripture. I was late here and have sat at the back alone, in my own horrible world. I've never sat and text someone in church but I've text Addison, telling her about what my Dad said about cancer and that it's making me want to try to walk in God's way. I don't think she likes it, she's told me that I'm brainwashed, I'm going to hurt myself by keeping this bottled up.

Gregg and I embrace as we meet in the church hallway after the service.

"You look amazing Faith, I feel like I haven't seen you in so long." He smiles down at me, checking me out with those dreamy brown eyes. "Do you want to come to mine and we'll chill out then I can drop you home later babe?" This is just what I need, some time alone with Gregg. Will it fix everything? Maybe he'll make me see that he is for me after all. I need to appreciate what I have, he's an amazing guy.

"Of course I do, let's go before we get captured." I laugh and we walk hand in hand to Greggs sleek black Volkswagen Golf.

The car journey consists of Gregg talking about his day at work and the new group of young people he's working with. He's so passionate. It's one of the things I love most about him. I've escaped from my world of dreaded thoughts and locked myself into Gregg. He's all I'm thinking about. I glance over at him as I drive, I feel like I could erupt with tears at the thought of ever hurting him or even worse, breaking his heart. It doesn't bear thinking about; I know I can make this right, I know it's the devil. They say bad company corrupts good habits and maybe that's what's happened; maybe being around Addison has turned me into a bad person.

I slide my shoes and blazer off and crawl into Gregg's comfortably large king size bed. His room is nicely decorating for a man living alone with red and black tartan bed sheets and shiny black bedroom furniture. I bet his Mum decorated this for him. Gregg emerges from the bathroom in a pair of Calvin Klein shorts, his body. Wow. It's the perfect body for a man, muscular, tanned and smooth. He moves in beside me, I lay on my back and his leans over looking down at me.

"You know if anything is up you can talk to me Faith." I smile quickly, my heart racing, does he know? Why does he think something is up with me? Has she told someone?

I can't allow my mind to race any longer, I need it to stop.

"I know Gregg, nothing is up, I'm okay I've just missed you that's all." I lean in, kissing Gregg with passion, pulling his body towards mine, he follows my grasp. Maybe having this, having him will make it okay? Maybe that's what I need, I need to be intimate with Gregg and that will stop me thinking about Addison. I plead with my mind to stop thinking about her. I pull Gregg more, willing him on top of me, his breath quick as I run my hands all over his body, caressing his muscular frame. My dress rides up and I push myself up against him, this isn't me, I can't stop myself, I need this. I can feel his excitement through his shorts and I know it's wrong to drag him into sin but it will be best for us in the long run. This could save us, save me from my own insane mind.

I push Gregg forward and pull myself upright using his body, then slide my dress over my head. Gregg has never seen me in my underwear. I can see the shock and excitement on his face. "Wow, your body is incredible Faith." He lays me back down on the bed, slipping his hand round my back as he does so and unhooks my bra. I pull it off and let it fall on the floor.

"Are you sure about…" Gregg's words are soft, I can tell he's nervous and anxious.

"Shhh baby, I'm sure." I lean in kissing Gregg more as he runs his hands over my breasts. My nipples harden under his touch. I'm not nervous, I should be but I'm not. The only feeling I have is one of repulsion, this isn't right but it needs to be.

As Gregg kisses me softly and slides his hands over my body I grind my hips upward, pressing against his hard erection. I close my eyes and for a moment, it feels amazing because in my head it isn't him on top of me. It's her it's Addison, why is it her? I can't stand these mind tricks any more. I kiss Gregg with more passion now, my insides are screaming for this to stop. It's wrong, I don't want it, I want her.

"Make love to me Gregg," I pant in his ear as he moves his body slowly on top of mine.

"Are you sure? But Faith..,"

"Shhh, please Gregg," I plead with him. He drags my clothes off hurriedly. I now lie underneath him completely naked. I feel exposed. He looks at me, wanting reassurance. I feel sick to my stomach.

"Please don't stop Gregg..."

I don't know how long that lasted. Long enough that the disgust I felt before has now escalated into feeling worthless. It felt horrible, dirty. I can't even look him in the eye. I lie on my side and Gregg holds me in his arms spooning me. The touch of his body against mine is enough to make my skin crawl.

"I love you Faith..." I close my eyes, pretending I've fallen asleep. I can't speak to him. I don't want him touching me again. What have I done? What has she done to me?

I lay for hours, not moving an inch, my body frozen. I hear Gregg begin to breathe louder and once I know he's asleep I allow the tears I've been holding back since I got here to fall down my cheeks. For so long, I've thought about how perfect our first time would be, how we would be married, wanting to have a baby, in our own home, with candles and whatever else he surprised me with. This has been as cheap as one of those couples you see on American TV in the motels. I feel like I've given myself away, to someone I no longer love, to someone I can't stand touching me. I want Addison, I need her, I need her to hold me, to tell me it'll be okay, how can I tell her what I've just done with Gregg?

Chapter 15

As soon as my eyes open, I know Gregg isn't in bed with me and rather than missing him or having any want for him to be there, I'm glad he's gone to work. At least now I don't have to look at him. I feel sick to my stomach, flashbacks of last night litter my mind, his groans echo in my ears and the feeling I had when he was inside me is enough to make me run to the shower and scrub myself until I feel my skin is raw. Once I've rid myself of any evidence that last night ever happened I begin my daily sob, leaning against the glass panel in the shower and allowing my behind to fall to the floor.

"I am gay?" I whisper to myself, my body convulsing as I hysterically cry.

"I am gay?"

I sit on the edge of Gregg's bed, I contemplate phoning Shannon I need my friend but I can't. If I told her any of this, even that I had sex with Gregg she would be so disappointed and she should be. My behaviour mimics that of someone Shannon would sit and talk about, firing stones until they were buried beneath the weight of her judgement. I call the only person I know might actually begin to understand.

"Hey sweetie, how are you?" That compassionate voice makes me long for her presence almost instantly I feel a huge guilt for having sex with Gregg, why should I? I mean yes I should feel guilty because I've sinned but I shouldn't feel guilty like I've done something on Addison. I hold myself together, adamant that I'll get through the rest of the day without crumbing into another desperate state.

"I'm okay, I was just wanting to see you, are you working today?"

"I see, it's your lucky day, I'm off and I'm free." Addison's voice is cool and confident.

"Maybe I could pick you up and we could head out for the day?"

"Sure, you can show me some more of the Emerald isle."

I smile, not able to hide how much I want to see her. Maybe I won't tell her about last night, she doesn't need to know.

"Can you be ready in half an hour?" "I'll try my best, see you soon."

Addison slides her perfect self into my car, she's wearing blue skinny jeans today, I don't see her in them often but when I do my eyes are glued to her behind like a hawk. She's wearing an oversized navy and red checkered shirt with red converse boots. Her familiar smell makes me feel at home again. As if she can read my face and tell that I've been craving her touch she leans over pulling me into a warm embrace. I sigh deeply as she holds me, stopping any tears that might be tempted to fall.

"You give the best hugs you know, it must be an American thing," I giggle as I start the car and begin to drive.

"Yea, I don't hug many people, so you should count yourself lucky." She teases.

"I was thinking, I'll take you to Newcastle, it's a bit of a drive but it's worth it?" I glance over, smiling, though I'm unable to make eye contact. I need to tell her about last night.

"Yea, Newcastle, that sounds like a plan. Is everything okay?" Why can she read me like a large print book? I've only been with her a few minutes and I've been actively hiding all expression that would give away my secret. Another secret, I hate secrets.

"There's something I need to tell you, I feel ashamed, so please don't judge me." I can feel Addison's eyes burning on me, I can't dare to look at her for fear that I'll crumble, no tears today I remind myself.

"Okay Faith, I've told you, you can tell me anything, I'll never judge you." I take a deep breath.

"I went to church last night and after I thought to myself, maybe I'm not gay, maybe it's the devil trying to deceive me, and I needed to know. I needed to prove to myself that it wasn't right, that Gregg wasn't right for me, I stayed with him last night." I glance over barely making eye contact, Addison looks like she's pitying me, or empathising, I don't know.

"Okay…" Just say it Faith, tell her what you done and tell her why there is shame written all over your face. A single tear rolls down my cheek.

"I had sex with him."

Addison doesn't jump to judge or reply with an answer that'll take away all of my qualms. Instead she reaches her arm over and rubs the back of my neck and shoulders as I drive, caressing me softly. I want to lie back into her touch, to recline my seat and try and fit us both together, just be held.

"I'm sorry you've had to do that Faith but you can't beat yourself up, at least you know now, you know it's true and it's who you are, now you can start your journey of accepting that." Every word draws me in, it's like she's a trained shrink, knowing what to say and how to say it to keep my fears at bay. I don't feel condemned, I know if I told anyone else this, any of the Christian people I know they would only multiply my feelings of shame and unworthiness.

***

We arrive in Newcastle after a long car journey. I loved every second of it, I don't care that back home my life is an absolute mess. All I care about is being with her. She's my escape, my solitude. She's the only thing I feel sure of right now. I love hearing about her life, she's told me that she's never known her Dad, sometimes she wishes she did, other times she feels she is better off without him. If he'd have wanted to know her he would be there. It's sad that she's had to go through that, she comes across as such a happy person with not a care in the world but really, she has scars just like everyone else. She's just better at coping than most people. She's told me about how much she misses her Mum and that losing her, she's lost part of herself, I can't imagine how that must feel, I try to be encouraging but deep down I know nothing I say will make that any better.

I park outside an old arcade with all of those flashing lights in the window, tempting you in, it reminds me of being a child and always wanting to go in and play with the other kids, Dad would never allow me, he said they were satanic, gambling, it's a sin, even if it is in 2ps, a slippery slope they say.
"I love the arcade, is this where we're going?" She beams.
"We can go wherever you want." I smile, finally able to make eye contact again with her and I realise how much I've missed those blue eyes, I feel like she can see straight to my soul.

We've decided that our first venture should be a machine you sit on and look up a massive screen while it takes you on a virtual roller coaster tour. "Are you sure you want to do this? It looks a bit scary." Addison keeps a straight face, playing with me, I laugh.

"Have a little faith in me." I joke as I lie back on the chair. We select our city, we've decided to go on the New York ride, and Addison is going to give me a tour. The rollercoaster is more like one of those annoying wonky seats you get landed with if you're last to sit at the table in a restaurant, apart from the loud crashing noises and flashing images in front of us. Addison lets out playful screams, she really doesn't care about people looking at her or what anyone thinks and I love that about her.

Next we decide we should document our day in one of those comic strip photo booths, we put our money in, then realise the seat is far too low and you can barely see the tops of our heads, the camera begins to flash and we both pop our heads up laughing hysterically. The photos are great, we managed to get a posing smile one and a funny face one, the rest show us laughing as we try and get ourselves into the frame. Looking at the photos makes me realise that no matter what is happening elsewhere, when I'm with Addison I am happy. I never feel alone when I am with her, why is that? I know I like her, more than I maybe should, does she just see me as a friend?

We spend hours in the arcade, wasting our money in silly machines to try and win cheap prizes. I've discovered that the ones one with the teddies are a fix, the claw just keeps opening, Addison says everyone knows that but she's adamant she isn't leaving without one as she puts another pound in the machine. Lifting up the Paddington Bear, he's coming, he's coming. She jumps in the air with excitement as after piling about £20 into the machine she's won a teddy worth about £5. I laugh out loud at the way she gets on then she turns to me, holding him out. "He's for you." Our eyes meet and I feel my cheeks blush, if it's possible for someone to actually warm your heart then she's warmed mine, giving me butterflies in my tummy as she does. All of a sudden Paddington Bear has become priceless, he'll be a forever reminder of happy she makes me.

"Awk you're so sweet. Thank you." I take my bear and squeeze him playfully.

As the day goes on I feel more at ease, when Addison touches my arm or places a hand on my back, I get a rush up my spine, but it feels normal, it feels right. I feel as though we've literally been on a rollercoaster ride, jam packed with excitement. We've done childish things and acted like kids but we're connecting somewhere, somehow. I don't know if she feels the same or if I'm taking her the wrong way. I could never bring myself to ask or to do anything that would indicate I like her more than just a friend. The fear of rejection is too much.

I don't want our day to end, I don't want my escape to end, why can't we just rent a caravan down here and stay forever. I dream away in my head about never having to face up to the reality of life and the fact that if I think the last while has been hard, I'll need a reality check when I finally come clean about how I feel inside to my family and friends. It doesn't bare thinking about.

"We should go and get a wee poke and sit in front of the water, you can't come to Newcastle without doing that." I smile as we finally leave the arcade.

"A wee what? A poke?" Addison laughs as she pokes my sides flirtatiously, I laugh, grabbing her hand to stop her from poking me, she keeps a hold of my hand, I feel my cheeks blush and the rush spreads all through my body like wildfire. "You know what I mean, whatever you American's call it, an ice cream."

***

As I pull up outside Sandra's house the weight of the burden feels like it's slipping slowly back onto my weak and broken shoulders.

"You've shown me a really good time today girl, I'm impressed." Addison looks at me intently, biting her bottom lip as she smiles. My eyes are glued to her lips. I want so much to kiss her. I want to feel how soft they are, I want them all over me. I'm craving her touch, her affection. I almost have to snap myself out of a day dream, like I've been glaring open mouthed at Addison's sweet pink lips.

"I'm glad you had fun, I can't wait to see you again." I look down a little as I speak, still feeling nervous to speak my mind around her, I don't have the confidence she has.

"I can't wait either Faith, you know, I really like you. I'm always here when you need me." She's said she likes me, what does she mean? Does she just like me as a friend or as more? Does she feel the same as me? What do I feel?

"I really like you too." I blurt out before my brain has time to throw up a million barriers. Her smile is wide and her eyes soft, she leans forward, my heart thumps rapidly, her face close to mine. I swallow hard. She embraces me, holding me tight for a few minutes, I never want her to let go.

CHAPTER 16

There was a time in my life when being at the prayer meeting uplifted me, gave me a renewed strength and cast aside any of my troubles. Church in general used to do that for me, Christian people used to do that for me. Things are changes, I'm different from them, I no longer feel that I belong here, with people who think I belong in the hottest part of hell. It'd like the devil is reserving a spot just for me because I'm falling for someone who happens to be a woman. Am I falling for her? If I am, I'm falling fast and I need her to catch me.

"Well babe, are you going to come and stay with me tonight?" Gregg asks with a sweet smile as the prayer meetings ends. I need to tell him, I can't look him in the eye. He's going to know I'm hiding something from him. I need to tell him tonight.

"Yea, I can't stay late though."

The drive to Gregg's house is dull and boring, he won't stop going on about football. I honestly don't care. I switched off ten minutes ago, I'm thinking about Addison, she's out tonight and she's going back to that gay bar. I wonder if she's meeting that woman again. Is she going to sleep with her? The thought of her with someone else sends my mind into overdrive. Why do I hate the thought of her with someone else when I have a boyfriend? We're just friends. Maybe I am going mad, it can't be normal to think like this. Gregg is so caught up in what he's saying that he doesn't even notice my terrified expression, terrified that Addison will find someone else while I'm stuck here with him. I need to speak to him.

He's going to know something is wrong.

"Are you looking forward to your weekend away this week? Dad was telling me about it." I ask as we walk into Gregg's house.
"Aye I can't wait Faith, it'll be nice to get a break, but I'll miss you." He puts his arms around my waist as we walk into the living room. I don't want him touching me, his touch is no longer a comfort but a reminder of who I really am, what I really want. Gregg sits down on the couch and pulls me onto his knee, my legs spread, knees at each side of his and I can tell he's in a playful mood. I couldn't feel more uncomfortable.

Gregg keeps trying to lure me into kissing him, I know what he wants, I've shown him that I'll have sex outside of marriage and now he wants more. Just like all of those sinners he judges. He has no chance. He kisses my lips and I allow him to, kissing him back with as much personality as a grape. I am willing it to end. His hands slide up my sides. He's giving me the creeps. I can't stop thinking about Addison. She's glued to the forefront of my mind. How would it feel to kiss her? To have her touch me, I know I would love every second of it, I would never want it to end and I'd never be able to think about anything else.

I pull my face away from Gregg, hoping he'll get the hint and stop kissing me. He sees it as an invitation to kiss my neck. Rather than the butterflies in my stomach I should be getting it feels like someone has let a hundred wasps loose inside me. The pain, the sting, my heart is sore. I feel so bad for him, he has no idea. His hands are on my waist and he's rocking my body back and forth, I can feel his erection under me. That's enough, I can't do it anymore.

"Gregg stop." He stops immediately, looking into my eyes lovingly.

"I'm sorry, I thought because we already have?" He says softly. I shake my head and take a deep breath.

"That was a mistake. You know it's wrong to do this before we're married. I should go. I'm sorry."

I make it to the front door before Gregg catches up with me.

"Don't rush off like that Faith, I'm sorry, I should have more respect." He embraces me, holding me tightly under his manly frame. The smell of his aftershave is a far cry from the intoxicating perfume that Addison wears. Why am I comparing everything about him to her? It's because I want her. I know it is. I accept that for tonight I've been defeated and my secret will weigh me down for another day.

"Don't be sorry Gregg, it's my fault. I'll see you before you go away?" Gregg lands a soft kiss on my lips.

"Yes you will princess."

***

I drove by Sandra's house to see if any lights were on, maybe Addison had come home from her night out. The house was in darkness. I'm lying in bed, scribbling in my diary, I could text and ask how her nights going, that's normal isn't it? If she wanted to talk to me surely she would have sent me a message. Leave the girl alone Faith, she's not your girlfriend, you have a boyfriend, what are you doing? My mind has been halved, like I have some sort of split personality disorder. One half of my brain is crying out for things to work with Gregg for us to have our perfect life together, the other half is coming to terms with the fact that I'll never have that perfect life because I'm different. Maybe my idea of perfect is warped. Maybe there's another perfect out there for me. I begin to write, I need these thoughts out of my head I will burn the page after if I have to.

This claxon is sounding in my mind, Are the blind just leading the blind? Can I really leave it all behind?
The signs are flashing for all to see. Maybe that life just wasn't for me? But does this mean I'll never be free?
The voices are screaming inside my head. The thoughts are so full of dread.
Is that dream I once had dead?
The flashes are changing my perception. Does that life have an attraction?
Can I even bare to look at my reflection? This whole time have I believed,
in something I've never been received? Is this pain just me grieving?
Were any of God's words ever true? Did he create those skies so blue?
Or is it a tale for fools like me and you? Will I ever get that faith again?

Has my hope been forever slain? Did Jesus really suffer my pain?

***

Its past midnight now and I still can't sleep. I can't get Addison out of my mind. I've looked through practically every photo she ever posted on Facebook and it only makes me pine for her more. I want to be inside her head, I want to know what she thinks about when she thinks of me, does she

have the same longing?
-Hey Addison, how's your night going? Xox

My phone buzzes and I answer immediately, my heart races like a horse in the last leg of the Grand National, skipping beats as it pleases. "Hey"

"Hi Faith, I'm just home, I thought I'd call you, I'm too drunk to be texting." Her laugh makes me smile, I'm also smiling that she's home, it doesn't sound like there's anyone with her and that gives me relief.

"So, what the crack, how was your night?"

"It was good yea, there are way too many drinks offers on in that bar, I couldn't help myself. What have you been doing apart from missing me?" There's that confidence, one of the things I love or like most about Addison. I giggle. I can practically hear her smiling down the phone. "I was just at the prayer meeting, then I went
over to Gregg's house for a bit, I wanted to talk to him about how I feel but I couldn't" My tone lowers, the defeat evident.

"It'll be harder the longer you leave it Faith, I know it's going to be hard but I'm here for you." "It's just, I know we're not meant to be and that's not his fault, I don't want to hurt him."

"I know you don't sweetie but it's for the best." I let out a loud sigh.

"I'm scared I'm going to lose everyone Addison, everyone is going to hate me."

"No they won't, things are never as bad as they seem and even if everyone does hate you, I like you enough to make up for that." Her words give me a wide smile.

"You really like me that much?" Maybe if she's drunk she'll tell me, I can't believe I just asked that, the silence is killing me, it's momentary but feels like an eternity.

"I haven't stopped thinking about you since the day and hour we met in Harmony Faith. I thought I was falling for another straight girl." Oh my goodness. How do I reply to that? Anxiety ripples through my body like this is all becoming real. Does she actually mean that?

How can I feel so anxious yet so excited at the same time?
"You're just saying that because you're drunk, we should talk when you're sober." I laugh, trying to make light of what is becoming an awkward conversation for me.
"No, this isn't drink talk. I think about you all the time Faith." I feel like I could cry, I don't know why, I'm just overwhelmed with emotion, is it good emotion or bad emotion? I think it's good. My confidence has slipped away beneath her compliments and face is like a hot coal.
"I think about you too Addison." I swallow hard. I can't believe I'm saying this, is this real?
"You need to be honest with Gregg." Gregg, why does he have to be in the picture? Why can't I just shake him off and we can run off together forever.
"I will be, soon, I promise." I know I have to be, I have no choice, I can't keep betraying home, every time I think about her I'm betraying him, he doesn't deserve that.
"Okay babe, remember I'm always here, I must go, and I'll call you tomorrow?" Her voice soft and soothing and I wish more than anything that she was beside me.
"I'll look forward to your call, bye Addison."

That really just happened. I just told her how I felt. This is real. This is my life. Everything I've come to know is no longer. How can I feel so strongly about someone I've only known for such a short while? How can she feel the same? What am I going to do about Gregg and my family? I feel like I should run away, she could take me to New York and I'd never have to face the shame.

CHAPTER 17

I arrive home from my Uni classes about 5pm, they dragged on and I was so distracted that I wouldn't be able to remember half of what was said. My last assignment in order to graduate is just a few weeks away and frankly, I couldn't care less. My mind is no longer my own, the guilt I feel for dragging Gregg along like this is unbearable. I don't want to tell him before his weekend away. It will ruin it for him. I've decided I'll tell him next week.

Addison hasn't called me today, just text me to say she's hungover and doesn't want to move from bed, lucky her. I wish I could be tucked up beside her. We haven't discussed what we talked about last night, I'm too scared to bring it up I think she was drunk last night and probably doesn't even remember saying it, let alone mean any of it. I can't keep being out of the house; my parents are going to start asking questions. Shannon has barely been in touch either and I'm sure it's because Gavin is filling her days, though I'm happy for her and I guess at the minute I don't really want to see her because I'm afraid she'll be able to tell there's something up with me.

Mum and I relax in the living room, she tells me about her weekend away this week with the girls, the men in church decided they'd treat themselves the same weekend but the women are heading to London, the men to Glasgow. Mum's excited and I like that, she deserves to be happy. I wish so much I could tell my Mum how I feel, sometimes you just need your Mummy and although mine is sitting a few feet away from me, I feel like we're a million miles apart. She would never accept me. She would hate me for bringing shame to her family.

The door swings open about 6:30pm and slams shut just as quickly. Dad storms into the living room and his face is red with anger. Here we go again. A bad day at work and he's come home to kick the cat, the cat being my Mum. She'll take it like she always does.

"Marj, you spent £300 today, what on?" He screeches, spitting his words at her like she is vermin. Dad watches his online banking like some sort of maniac, when he goes in a bad mood he'll go through every transaction, how can he love money so much when the Bible is so against that. Mum stands up, I don't like how this is going. I stand up beside my Mum, something I've never done before.

"Liam I told you I had to tax the car and do the shopping for the month." Mum says softly, basically cowering below him.
"Bullshit, there's no way that cost £300, you're making a mug out of me, I'll take that card off you." My Mum is visibly upset and terrified her small frame almost trembling.

"Why don't you let Mum go and get a job instead of keeping her locked up? Then she wouldn't have to spend 'your' money and you wouldn't scream at her every day?" I don't know where those words came from. My Dad's eye meet mine, he's like a rattlesnake, ready to pounce. Mum looks at me in a state of shock. My hands shake with fear, inside I am proud. I need to stand up for my Mum, once and for all.
"Don't you dare speak to me like that you wee bitch." Dad scowls.

"Get to your room." He points his finger towards the doorway.

"I'm 23. You can't send me to my room anymore, leave my Mum alone." Dad takes a step toward me and Mum places a hand on his chest.

"Faith honey just go to your room please?" she pleads with me, a tear streaming down her cheek. "You don't pay a penny here either and you drive about in a car that I bought you, you're just like your Ma." I like that he thinks I'm like my Mum and he can take the car, I don't care.

"I'd much rather be like my Mum than a monster like you."

My Dad's blue eyes are cold like ice, a stark comparison to the beetroot coloured anger showing on his face. I swallow hard expecting my Dad to scream at me so loudly he will bust my ear drums but his response isn't verbal, instead he lifts his hand at lightning speed and with the back of it knocks me off my feet. The sting on my face is unbearable and I cry out in agony. My Mum's screeches have no bearing on my Dad. He towers over me. My nose feels like it's been broken, tears from the pain stream down my face. I won't let him win, I've snapped. Enough is enough. I pick myself up off the floor, the blood pours from my nose.

"You're a big man, hitting a girl. Well done." I clap my hands now covered in blood sarcastically at him.

The mighty man of God turns on his heels and storms out of the house. My Mum is in shock, she is physically shaking, tears stream from her eyes. She grabs me hugging me.

"Faith, are you okay? I'm sorry, I'm sorry." I hug my Mum tight, trying not to get blood on her white blazer, my efforts fail.

"I'm fine Mum. It's not your fault. You need to leave him, please. You can't stay with that any longer." My Mum rushes to the kitchen bringing me a tea towel to hold my nose.

"Faith he's my husband, your Father, you know I can't do that." I shake my head at my Mum, tears fall from my eyes, knowing how trapped she must feel.

"I've got to get changed Mum." The blood has soaked my grey and white t-shirt. I didn't know a nose even held so much blood.

I lean my back against the wall in my room, staring in the mirror, every emotion under the sun welcomes itself into my mind and I foolishly allow it. I slide down the wall, clutching my knees as I sit on the floor. My nose starting to throb now, I can see the swelling in the mirror. I bow my head. My Dad hasn't hit me for a few years now, right up until I was maybe 19 he would discipline me because that's what the Bible says you have to do. If he didn't slap me like today then he would whip me with his belt. When I became an adult he seemed to focus on my Mum more. I always felt guilty, before we had shared the burden and then I left it all for her.

I lie in bed, in my familiar foetal position, I can't even bring myself to pray, what's the point, I've been praying for years that God would stop my Mum being abused but apparently God was otherwise engaged. Addison has been trying to call me but I've been too embarrassed to answer, worried that she'll know something is wrong and make me tell her. She has a way with words, when she asks my heart just pours out to her. I can't speak to her. I just need to be alone. My mind twos and froes like a bobbing buoy in the ocean and close my eyes hoping I'll wake up without a broken nose.

Chapter 18

It's Friday morning, I've avoided contact with the outside world until now, cooping myself up in my bedroom and pretending that I was poorly. I couldn't have anyone seeing my coal black nose or swelling that surrounds it. Mum and Dad are both packing for their weekends away and Gregg wants to see me before he goes. He hasn't stopped texting me, wanting to see me but I can't allow him, I feel so bad, he must be so confused. He has to be he is telling me how he feels closer to me now than ever before, that he wants to spend his life with me. It's like I'm paying my karma for stringing him along and I deserve it. Dad leaves early to take Mum to meet her friends, Mum hugs me and tells me to be safe for the next few days. Dad doesn't look at me. He hasn't since he smashed my face in. They look like the perfect married couple, Dad helping Mum into the car with her cases, Mum waves me off and they smile and laugh together. How looks can be so deceiving.

I sort some washing out and head upstairs to put my clothes away. My bed beckons me and I lay on top of the covers, breathing out deeply. Feeling relieved that I can be alone for the next few days. Shannon has text me asking if I want to come over to watch a movie tonight, I wish I could, I can't have her seeing me like this. I've even locked the front door in case she decides to call unexpectedly. She should know, everyone should know what a monster my Dad is, like I've learned myself though, you can only keep a mask on for so long, eventually it'll be dragged off or fall off when you least expect it. I can't stop playing the same song, like the words were made up just for me. Did Adele have me in mind when she wrote A Million Years Ago? I doubt it but it certainly feels like it. I've never had a song that touched me to my very core. I blast it so loud I barely hear the sound of the niggling voice in my head which tells me I'm going to hell. Have I finally found a way to silence it?

"I miss the air, I miss my friends, I miss my Mother, I miss it when, life was a party to be thrown but that was a million years ago." – Adele – Million Years Ago.

-Hey Faith, I've tried to call you a few times, I know your parents and Gregg are away, maybe we could hang out tonight? Xx A

I wish so much I could see Addison tonight, have her come and stay with me and provide that solid ground my mind is dreaming of but I can't. I can't have her know my Dad is a monster. I'm ashamed of myself and of him.

-I'm just wanting some alone time at the minute, my head is all over the place but maybe we could get together during the week? I do miss you Xoxo

-Are you okay? I'm worried about you, you haven't been yourself the past few days. I know times are hard, but it's all going to be okay, I promise. I miss you too. I can't stop thinking about you Xx A

Maybe some makeup would cover my swollen nose? No, it wouldn't who am I kidding? My heart is aching for her. She can't stop thinking about me. Those are the sweetest words I feel I've ever heard because likewise I can't get her off of my mind. I have a free house all weekend and she could be here every minute of it, that's what I'd been planning before my Dad decided to ruin everything. Was it even worth standing up for my Mum if she stands by him?

-I will be okay. I'll give you a call later sure. Enjoy the rest of your shift.

I can't stop thinking about you either Xoxo
-Faith promise me that you'll come to me if you need someone? I don't
want you to go through this alone? Xx A

I can't promise that to Addison because I need someone now but I can't have her here.

***

I wake to the sound of the doorbell; I came downstairs in the afternoon to watch some TV and must have fallen asleep. It's dark outside. How did I sleep so long and who is at my door? I can't answer it, what if it's Shannon and she sees my face? The unknown visitor is now knocking on the door. Who knocks a door when there's a doorbell? I'm rigid on the sofa, too afraid to move in case they see me through the living room window. My phone buzzes on the arm of the couch, whoever is outside must be phoning me. It's Addison.
"Hello?"
"Faith I've been worried sick, are you okay?" "Why? Yea I just fell asleep, sorry."
"I'm outside."

I open the front door slowly, hoping the dimly lit hall will hide the state of my face. It's more bruising now than swelling. I still look like I've done a few rounds with Carl Frampton.
"Faith, what's happened to your face?" The colour drains from Addison's face, her eyes wide as she walks into the hall. I close the door behind her.
"I'm sorry. I didn't want you seeing me."

"Is it Gregg? What has that bastard done? I'll kill him."
"No, no it's not Gregg. Please just leave it Addison." I walk

into the living room and she follows me, I can hear her breathe deeply as if to try and calm herself down.

"I won't leave it, who done this to you?" Addison is getting angry, her fiery side showing as she sits beside me on the couch. I make eye contact with her, eventually. Those amazing blue eyes, she's flawless. I stay silent, disengaging my brain from her questions and instead admiring her beauty. Wow.

"Tell me, who done this to you?" She pulls me out of my trance. I look to the floor awkwardly, ashamed. I have to tell her, I can't lie to her face. "It was my Dad." I swallow the lump that's made its way into my dried up throat. She shakes her head in disbelief, the rage evident on her face.

"Can we just not talk about it please?" I plead with her, not wanting to deal with the reality anymore. She's here and she's my escape, I don't care about my face anymore, only hers. She continues shaking her head. I feel her soft hand on my cheek as she wipes away an escaped tear. "If he hurts you again, I will kill him."

Her touch is sending shockwaves up my spine, I've been craving it so much, I need her. I feel like she's all I have left. She moves her hand onto mine and holds it firmly, her hands cold from the evening air. I place my other hand on top of hers to try and warm them, rubbing them gently. I lay my head on the back of the sofa and turn my head to face her, she does the same. Her face close to mine, she gazes in my eyes, stirring up those feelings of lust deep inside of me. I move my eyes to her lips. They're so perfect, plump and kissable.

I don't know how long we've sat here, just staring into one another's eyes. The odd time one of us will give a slight smile and the other will mimic it causing some small giggles. I just feel at home with her. Nothing else in the world matters. My heart has found a comfortable pace of around a million beats per minute and my breaths are deep and loud. I can barely blink, her pupils are large and they outstare me at times, I have to look down slightly. I'm still so nervous around her, even though it feels so right. The anxiety just builds at times when the half of my brain trapped in church tells me I'm sinning. Addison moves her face slowly towards mine. I honestly think my heart has stopped beating. I hold her hand, tighter than before as my nerves bundle up. She gets around a centimetre from my face, I can feel my hands tremble but she holds them tight, reassuring me. I can feel her warm breath on my face. I have never wanted something so much in my life.

"I'm falling for you Faith." Addison whispers, I close my eyes breathing her in, taking in those words, I feel like my heart has melted inside of my chest. I'm falling for her too but I can't bring myself to speak. She moves her face slowly. Her lips gently brush off mine, almost as if she's testing the water, getting closer to me. I keep my eyes closed and allow her to brush her lips off mine again, I almost gasp out loud at her soft touch.

Addison lands a soft kiss on my lips. I open my mouth slowly, allowing her soft lips to meet mine again. A gentle squeeze of my hand, to tell me I'm okay, I know I'm okay, I've never felt so complete in all my life. Addison and I kiss slowly, the type of kiss I've never experienced before. It feels like there are fireworks going off in my heart and a million butterflies in my tummy. It feels like something out of the movies, she reaches her hand up and strokes my face. Kissing me again, sliding her warm tongue to meet mine, I feel warmth between my thighs and a deep longing for her. She can probably feel my hands trembling and I've no doubt that makes her stop kissing me, she moves her face back from mine. Lifting her arm up and ushering me to come in to her, I rest my head under her arm and she holds me tight. I feel completely overwhelmed, my mind, my body, every part of me. As I hold onto her body tightly, one arm around her back, the other around her stomach. I look down and watch as a tear falls from my face, almost in slow motion and lands on her black jeans.

CHAPTER 19

Addison and I lay silently on the couch together for ages, though it felt like a few minutes to me. She isn't like Gregg, she's gentle. She strokes my hair, pays attention to the parts of me that aren't just designed to turn me on. The silence speaks a thousand words, I've never felt so at home than when she's holding me, she's the missing part of my jigsaw piece I've been searching for, for so long. She offers to go home one last time before we walk up the stairs, I think she's scared of putting pressure on me or overstaying her welcome. She could never overstay her welcome. I give her some pyjamas, I really wanted to choose skimpy ones but I was too embarrassed so I settled on plain old navy and pink tartan ones. I set them on the bed for her, and take my own into the bathroom to get changed. I feel too awkward to change in front of her, even though she's a girl and it wouldn't normally matter. It's different.

We sit up in bed, with just a dim side lamp on. I didn't bother to switch on the TV because I know neither of us have any interest at all.

"Do you believe in God Addison?" I ask curiously.

"Yea I guess I believe there's something out there but I don't believe in organised religion, why?" She speaks in a serious tone, I like that. She can be hilarious but at the same time genuine and caring.

"I don't know, I just wondered if you ever felt guilty for being gay." I can see the shock on her face, all of the sudden what

I've just asked sinks into me as well. Surely that's a crazy thing to ask someone. There's a slight laugh before she answers.

"No, I've never felt guilty but then nobody ever told me it was wrong, you've been told that for so many years that it'll take time before those feelings erode, but they will and I'll help you through it, every step of the way." My face lights up at her encouraging words, rather than putting me down for asking a question that might have offended her, she shows understanding and compassion. Two characteristics almost every other person around me is lacking.

I'm losing myself in her eyes as we speak to each other, open conversations, with points to debate, unlike any other conversation I ever have where the bottom line lies in the Bible. It's like she's opening my mind to a whole new way of thinking. There's just something about this girl. I'm so drawn to her, I could listen to her speak for hours on end, but for now I have other plans for those lips. My eyes keep wandering to them, I see her looking at mine also. I could never make the first move. I'd be way too embarrassed. Like a mind reader she leans in and lets me feel those lips on mine again. There's a massive explosion of emotion, I can't describe how incredible it feels. I kiss her back, slowly, sensually. We slide down the bed together, I lie on my back and she leans over me, kissing my forehead, then my nose, she makes me giggle. Her bright smile, I need it framed and on my wall for when I have a bad day. Her lips meet mine and it's like a rush of electricity through my veins, I have flashbacks of the morning I touched myself right here, thinking about her.

Addison continues to kiss me, our kiss becomes more heated, the taste of her mouth is like an addiction as we let our tongues collide, exploring each other. Her hand glides up my thing, making me wriggle underneath her. She continues to allow her tongue to explore my mouth. I try and keep focused on our kiss but her hand is distracting me, making its way up to my pelvic bone, she slides it underneath my top, allowing her fingers to explore my now exposed stomach. I'm so nervous. I feel like my insides are shaking, I place my hand on her neck as she kisses me, letting my nails glide along her skin. Her kiss though more heated, still giving me butterflies. I run my hand down her neck, past her shoulder and onto her side, dangerously close to her breasts, I bet they're as perfect as I imagined, I don't think she's wearing a bra. I feel her move her mouth off mine, landing soft kisses on my cheeks until she reaches my neck, the touch of her hot wet lips on my neck set my body on fire, the heat between my legs increasing with every breath. Her lips reach my ear and she bites softly on my earlobe, paying all the right parts of me attention. Her hand moves up my skin and land on my breast through my bra, she begins caressing me, her hot breath in my ear making me moan out with pleasure.

I can feel Addison's heart rate increasing as I follow her lead, allowing my hand to slide onto her breast over her top. She has no bra on, I can feel her hard nipple under my hand, I have images of running my tongue over it, feeling it harden as I do. I feel her, pulling me forward off the bed, she undoes my bra and pulls my top off within seconds. My cheeks are flushed. I look up into her eyes, my hand still on her breast as her nipple hardens. She pulls her top off without hesitating. Her breasts are just as I imagined. Her nipples are dark and edible.

She moves herself on top of me, one leg in between mine, holding herself up with her toned arms. She kisses my lips, this time a little more rough, with more lust. I kiss her back eagerly, as she presses her body against mine, making me moan. Her hand slides over my breast and my nipple hardens, she plays with it, making it feel sensations I've never felt before. I can barely handle it, she grinds down on me more, she's barely touching me but my moans are becoming louder. She holds herself up with those perfect arms again and in doing so presses her heat firmly against my throbbing clit. I can barely keep my eyes open as I moan out in pleasure. She moves her face towards my exposed nipple, breathing on it, all the while looking up at me with those intimidating eyes. Her tongue comes out of her mouth and she begins to lick my nipple, playfully, watching my reaction as she does. She begins to lick faster. Then she places my whole nipple in her mouth and begins sucking and nibbling on it.

My back arches and I force myself up against her, this makes her grind down on me more, I don't break eye contact the whole time, I can't, it's like I'm transfixed on her. She lifts herself up again moving her body back and forward on top of mine, her nipples close to my face, I stop looking at her, to stare at them, so close to me. I want so much to kiss them, lick them. Like she can see into my thoughts she moves her body. She holds her nipple in front of my mouth and then places a hand on the back of my head and presses my mouth against her. I begin to kiss them, softly. She holds the back of my head, not allowing my mouth to move from her nipple, I look up into her eyes and she begins moving faster and faster on top of me. I moan loudly onto her nipple, she must love it because she moans out in pleasure with every touch of my tongue.

My body is trembling, I'm feeling like I'm about to explode

underneath her, she moves, pressing her lips firmly against mine, kissing me with heat, our breaths quicken together. She moans into our kiss, I can feel my body, I can't take it any longer. The wetness between my legs is too much, I jolt back and forward, arching my back, she moves, looking straight into my eyes, she keeps pushing herself harder and faster against me until my body erupts with pleasure and hers does the same. The touch of her against me makes me almost scream as I feel my body give into her. She breathes deeply landing one last kiss on my lips and lets her body fall on top of mine.

Chapter 20

I wake on my side, Addison's is spooning me, she has one arm under my head and I'm holding her hand, her other is tucked underneath my tummy. Our bodies pressed together, I can feel her skin on mine and it's the best feeling in the world. I know by her breathing that she's still asleep so I lay still. I can't believe how amazing I feel, like I've woken up to a completely different life, where I am me, not just someone everyone else wants to see. Enjoying the escape, though I'm at home, I feel like I've travelled a million miles away, somewhere my troubles can't find me. I feel like I've travelled home in her arms.

I creep out of bed quietly, pulling my top on, looking down at her as she lays asleep, she's so perfect, even when she's sleeping. I want so much to wake her just to see her smile but that can wait. I make us some French toast and scrambled eggs and tea, using the tray my Mum uses for my Dad, to deliver his breakfast in bed. I stand over the bed.

"Morning Addison," I say, loud enough to wake her but not too loud that I'd startle her. She curiously lets her eyes open and there it is her million dollar smile.

"Honey, you're so sweet." She sits up in bed and I hand her the tray before crawling in beside her. I only realise I'm staring at her bare breasts when she reaches and grabs her top off the floor. "Now, now Faith, that's dessert." She teases, as we share a laugh and tuck into our breakfast.

"Tell me how you feel this morning Faith?" Her sexy

American tone ripples through every inch of my body and causes my insides to stir.

"Thanks for the tea by the way, usually it's me serving you," she smiles as she takes a sip. That soft laugh, I stare at her plump lips as she smiles with those pearly white teeth. Today she looks more amazing than ever, her long brown hair is tied into a high messy ponytail, her skin is soft and tanned, blue eyes burning through me.

"I feel amazing this morning, how do you feel?" I still look down at times when I speak to her though my confidence is growing.

"I'm happy to be here with you, more than happy."

We finish our breakfast and I clear away our dishes, crawling back into bed beside Addison, my mind is forcing me to think about what might happen tomorrow? When my parents and Gregg are back and reality sets in. I don't want to think about it, I want to keep living in this little bubble.

"I don't know what to do, what am I supposed to do?" my voice sounds panicked as if I've suddenly realised that this is going to be traumatic. Addison wraps both of her arms around me, holding me tight. She presses her mouth against my hair.

"It's gonna be okay, I promise." She whispers softly.

"I don't know what to do Addison, I feel like I'm trapped, my mind is in constant agony every day, Gregg is more in love with me than ever, my Mum is miserable and putting on a mask for everyone else, my best friend doesn't notice enough to ask and my Dad's getting worse, I haven't been able to leave the house because of him, he hasn't spoken to me since." My words are broken up by my catching of small short breaths as I get a burn at the back of my throat along with

112

those lumps that stop you from speaking and when you do speak the tears just burst out, which is exactly what's just happened.

Addison swallows hard gazing down at me, she looks angry and confused.
"That's wrong, he can't do that. What sort of man..." her voice getting aggravated.
"Stop it's my fault I shouldn't have got involved." I cut her off.

"Stop blaming yourself Faith, for everything. None of this is your fault. Your Mum needs someone to defend her, he's obviously got control over her and she must feel trapped, just like you." That soft silky hand wipes my tears away once again, the touch on my skin makes me long for more, I don't want her to ever leave me. I feel safe with her. I breathe deeply, allowing my tears to fall. I try to pull myself together. I reach and take her hand off my face with mine, holding it and squeezing it tightly. I feel her squeeze back as she leans down and plants a soft peck on my forehead. Her breath on my skin makes my heart quicken. Her face is now dangerously close to mine and I can feel my body begin to tingle. All of my emotions are swept away except for the want of having her. I don't know how, I just want her. I want to feel last night all over again. Her pupils become enlarged and she keeps her face close to mine, gently squeezing on my hand as she rubs it gently with her thumb.

"You're so beautiful." Those words almost purred at me, make me shudder and blush, with everything going on in my mind, she can still make me feel good. How do I respond, my tongue is tied, I want to tell her that she's the most perfectly crafted being I've ever laid eyes on and how just being in her presence lifts my soul.

"So are you." My words are quiet and shy, my face reddens slightly more and I can she her lips stretch into a small smile, like she knows how difficult that was for me.

"For a minute forget about everything Faith, it's just us, here and now." Almost like a command I do as she says and my mind is rid of the anxiety, the guilt and all of the other emotions that have been polluting my life. Almost as if she's removed it all with a few simple words and a touch more caring than any I have ever felt before.

"Are you okay?" she asks softly. I nod reassuringly, my eyes now transfixed on her lips. I've never wanted someone more in my life. She lays me back on the bed, she moves her hand back to stroke my cheek softly, then she runs her thin warm finger to my earlobe caressing it slowly, sliding it teasingly down my neck, my very bones tremble as she runs her finger back up my neck and slides her hand under the back of my neck resting on the pillow. Using her hand on my neck she beckons me towards her, as she moves her face closer to mine. Our noses meet and she sweetly, moves hers from side to side slowly touching mine. The warmth of her breath on my lips gives me goosebumps. I feel her plant her soft perfectly crafted lips onto mine. The rush of heat down my body makes its way between my legs. I kiss her back slowly and softly, closing my eyes and allowing my body to feel every second of this. Our tongues meet as she glides hers gently into my mouth and I can sense my body craving her touch.

I don't want this kiss to ever end. I feel her sliding one leg in between mine as she moves on top of me, my heat now pressed against her thigh, which makes me jolt forward with excitement. I can barely breathe as we continue our passionate kiss. I lift a hand and slide it onto her perfectly curved side, pulling at her oversized t-shirt to bring her closer to me. That body on top of me, electrifying every muscle in my body as she grinds herself down on me. I begin to moan softly into our kiss and feel her do the same as I push my body back up against hers. My hands are wandering over her body on top of mine as she moves my head to the side and begins to kiss my neck, running her warm tongue over my skin, sucking and biting on my earlobe. Our bodies begin to move faster as she moans into my ear. I can feel my body yearning for more. I don't know how much I can handle. She has now slid herself between my legs and is pressing herself against me harder this time. Lifting her hips off and letting our bodies clash gently more rough and hard than last night. Her head raises and she looks in my eyes, my stomach has butterflies. I arch my back, my toes curling into my bed sheets. I let out a loud moan and my body feels like it's convulsing underneath her, my legs shake and I feel myself reach climax. Addison's body is doing the same and then she lands one last pressing push onto my body and then lays her head on my chest breathing heavily.

I've heard people in Uni talking about Orgasm and avoided their conversations, I assumed I had one when I had sex with Gregg, how wrong was I? That was the most amazing feeling in the world and we were both fully clothed. I can feel the warmth between my legs pulsating; I wrap my arms around Addison and hold her close to me.

***

We sleep in each other's arms until mid-afternoon, she wakes me, planting a soft kiss on my lips, enough to wake me and I automatically begin to kiss her back. I feel her hand run up my side slowly and gently, she tugs my top up exposing my side, she continues her fingers running over my smooth stomach area. Then she stops kissing me, looking deep into my eyes.

"If you want me to stop just tell me." I nod, her stopping is the last thing on my mind, she removes herself from my lips and uses my arm to pull me forward, in an instant she slips my top over my head, I feel bare and exposed but it feels right. Addison's eyes have stolen my mind, I'm transfixed, and she cautiously lifts a hand and runs it up my stomach, before leaning in to kiss my neck with her hot mouth. As I feel a hand slide over my exposed breast it sends waves of pleasure throughout my body. I wriggle a little, not because I'm uncomfortable but because I feel so amazing. My nipple hardens under her touch and she slowly kisses her way down my neck. I know what's coming and I can barely stop myself from pushing her head onto my breast. That tongue I long for so often runs around my areola and she sucks gently on my erect nipple. I feel my hips push upwards of the bed and I arch my back, one hand plays teasingly with my other breast and she licks and sucks me, forming an increasing heat between my legs.

My hands are frozen by my sides, I don't know what to do with them, I wish so much I could shake these nerves and make her feels how she makes me feel. Like a mind reader she stops for a moment and pull her vest top off, discarding it onto the floor then resumes pleasuring me. I feel her hand touch mine as she lifts it, leading it to her exposed breast, I look down and they're perfect, not that I've seen many but hers are pert and firm. She leads my hand to gently rub her, as she moans onto my nipple before giving it a gentle nibble. I don't want this feeling to ever stop, and there's no sign that it will. Addison lifts her head again and lands a peck on my lips. "Are you okay?" she asks in her caring tone. "I'm more than okay," I continue to caress her breast as I look as her, sliding her hardened nipple between my fingers. Addison has a serious look in her eye. She stands up off the bed and walks round beside me and uses my legs to turn me so that I'm facing her. Sliding her hands underneath me she tugs on my bottoms and pants off. I take a long lasting breath as I look down at her, she in now kneeling on the floor between my legs.

I'm completely naked, all of my imperfections exposed, she runs her hands up my legs and teases my inner thighs. My body is crying out for her, I need her.

"Don't stop." I moan as I bite on my lower lip. I feel one hand spread my legs farther, exposing my smooth bare sex. A soft kiss on my thigh with that tongue is enough to send shockwaves through my body, as I feel one of her fingers run slowly up the middle of my bare slit. My hips naturally press themselves up against her, wanting more. I grab hold of the bed sheets as I feel her finger slip to touch my inner lips. The moisture between my legs now begins to pour out of me.

"You're so wet Faith, I want to taste you." She purrs as she runs her tongue along my thigh, dangerously close to my sex. I breathe fast and my heart acts like it's developed some form of condition. It's beating so fast that it could almost beat out of my chest. Her warm tongue runs from the middle of my slit all the way up to my clit were she presses firmly making my body jolt under her. She does this enough that I can almost hear her lapping up my moisture. Her tongue has stopped on my clit and she begins to kiss it passionately, leaving no area untouched. Circular motions and then long hard licks, my body is beginning to sweat, I've never felt anything like this before in my life.

Just as I feel that my body cannot handle anymore, Addison moves her hand between my legs and without hesitation slides a long thin finger inside me, I grind upwards onto her tongue letting out a loud moan. Her fingers slides deep inside me, she slowly begins to form a rhythm of laying a firm lick on my clit every time her finger lands deep inside me. I'm now taking two of Addison's finger inside my sex, my breaths have turned into pants and my legs are trying to close as my body cripples under her. With one last deep hard finger into me she licks my clit rampantly, forcing me to explode in loud moans, my body shaking like convulsions. I can't speak only moan loudly, as she keeps her fingers inside me, moving it in such a way that she's touching something that hasn't been touched before, her licks are hard and fast now and my clit is pulsing on her tongue. Whatever she's touching is amazing, my body jerks and I scream with pleasure and with that, she knows to stop. My eyes are wide, my body is numb, I can't move, she lies down beside me and pulls me into her arms, holding me tightly.

CHAPTER 21

We've been watching random Netflix movies all day, she loves action movies and I'm happy to watch them as long as I'm with her. My body feels like it's been through a rigorous routine in the gym, I'm exhausted and she holds me, caresses me, kisses me at the right time in the right place. It's like she's my Saviour. She's saved me from living a lie, how long would I have continued for? I begin to open up more to Addison about when my feelings started, when I was in first year of high school. My first few teenage years were when I really started to understand what homosexuality was, most of the time I heard about it was in church, from that time I was told how disgusting it was, that there was nothing worse. Other times were in the school playground when one boy said he was gay and he got bullied for it, I think he started to self-harm after that and his parents moved him school. I didn't dare tell anyone about the feelings I had been having towards girls in my life because I was scared. I was most scared that if I said it, it would make it more real and God would punish me, sending me to eternal damnation. I managed to keep those feelings suppressed for years until I noticed Addison at Harmony and something just set them off.

I share my experiences of growing up in a family where my Dad is looked at as the perfect gentleman, involved in all aspects of church, a successful local security firm owner and the perfect husband. When really I've had to listen to years of abuse, locking myself in my bedroom as a child, listening to my Mum being thrown about like a ragdoll by the man she would give her life for. Yet I would listen when my parents friends from church came over and they would gossip about other members of the church and how they weren't walking in God's way. My Mum always acted like the abuse never took place, she only tried to stop it when my Dad first hit me as a child but her efforts were in vain.

Addison opens up about her Mum passing away and how it's turned her life upside down, she has felt like there's a gaping hole in her life that will never be replaced, her Mum was her best friend. Hearing that she's hurting makes my heart feel sore, Sandra had told me it was unexpected but that her Mum was suffering from cancer, Addison doesn't go into detail. I hear of her ex-girlfriend that cheated on her while she was caring for her Mum when her health deteriorated badly in a short space of time and how she's worried it will be hard to trust again. After this Sandra begged and pleaded that she come and live with her, she was concerned as Addison hadn't been herself, she doesn't elaborate much on that but that she had no family left over there. We share our plans for our careers, Addison wants to study business again and eventually start up her own coffee shop during the day which turns into a bar/club at night time, and she said she got the idea from a Lesbian show she watched. I tell of how after my English degree I would like to qualify as a teacher and work in a High School. I feel as though she's really interested in my goals, I don't know that anyone's ever made me feel like that, normally people just say God has a plan for your life so live in his way and he'll show you.

We continue on for the rest of the evening, stopping only to have some pizza for dinner. We hold each other, kiss each other affectionately and build upon a connection I feel I've always longed for. Addison introduces me to stand-up comedy, we watch Kevin Hart on Netflix, and I laugh so hard my stomach hurts. It gets late and my eyes begin to tire, I switch the TV off and give Addison a warm smile.

"Can you stay tonight?" I ask shyly, still getting the butterflies in my tummy when I say such things to her.

"Sure, it'll be my pleasure sweetheart." She yawns, stretching. I just want to be held, all night long. With that I roll onto my side and she moves behind me, sliding one arm under my pillow and the other around my waist, pulling her body so she's pressed against mine, she lands a soft kiss on the back of my neck. I stroke her hand around my waist and hold it loosely, the perfect spoon, to end the perfect day.

CHAPTER 22

I wake early to the sound of my alarm, reaching to my bedside table to mute it. The sun is making its way through the middle of my curtains. I sit up in bed having a much needed stretch. I peer down at Addison who has paid no attention to the alarm and is still lying on her side with her arm over as if I'm still there. She looks just as amazing first thing in the morning. I don't. I don't want to leave her but I have to. Knowing our amazing weekend is coming to an end gives me a heavy heart.

I finally muster up the strength to take myself to the bathroom and have a shower, it's Sunday and I need to go to church this morning, I have to help Joyce with the Sunday school presentation that I've been preparing. I know I'd much rather have a repeat of yesterday but I can't let Joyce or the kids down. My nose is nowhere near as bad today, a few layers of foundation and I'll have my mask on just like everyone else at church. I have a sense of dread about going. I don't know how it's going to make me feel. Am I going to slip back into self-loathing, guilt? I shake off the feelings for now, it doesn't matter how it makes me feel, I can't control that, Addison told me everything is going to be okay and I trust in her. Though she won't be at church with me, what if I breakdown?

I get dressed and ready in the spare room, not wanting to wake Addison from her peaceful sleep. I opt for navy skinny chinos, with a maroon top and brogues, I pull on my thick grey coat. My long blonde hair sits in loose waves and I wear thick foundation on my swarthy skin, my eyebrows are perfectly sculpted and my lips noticeably pinkish. A slight touch of mascara around my bright blue eyes and I'm ready to go. I feel good today. I look like a weight has been lifted from my shoulders. Like all the weeks of tears have finally come to an end and I'm finding myself again but am I losing my faith in the process?

I know I have to wake Addison. I wish I could leave her in my bed and have her to come home to. I sit on the edge of the bed, reaching down and stroking her cheek with the back of my hand. "Good Morning." I whisper softly, not wanting to startle her. Her hand reaches out and touches my arm, her eyes unwillingly open slightly. When our eyes meet her perfect smile shows. "You look amazing." She gently squeezes my arm and sits up in the bed. I blush shyly, she's given me butterflies again and she's only spoken three soft words. I don't have to explain to Addison where I'm going or why she needs to leave. She knows it's Sunday and she doesn't force me to discuss it. That makes me like her even more. She stands off the bed, sliding her shoes on.

"Is it okay if I wear this home?" She giggles to herself. Knowing that putting her shoes on means I don't really have a choice, she'll be wearing my navy and pink tartan pyjamas and matching navy vest top home. Though I agree quickly because I know that she looks even better when she's wearing something of mine, I don't know why, she just does.

I'm almost overwhelmed with anxiety as Addison and I rush to my car, frightened that someone would see, Shannon or another neighbour? It's like reality kicks in again and I snap out of the trance I've been in from Friday evening. I push the thoughts aside and talk to Addison about how much I enjoyed our time together, she tells me the same and that she can't wait to see me again. As I pull up outside Sandra's house she pulls me in for a tight squeeze before landing a warm kiss to my lips which sends the warmth flying through my body. I kiss her back softly, forgetting about where I am, or who might see us.

"Have a good day sweetie and I'll see you soon."
"You too, yea I hope so." I beam, landing one last peck on her moist lips.

***

The feeling I got as I stepped into church was a far cry from 10 minutes previous when I felt on top of the world, like no one could ever take away my newly found happiness. My whole body feels like it's been drenched in guilt, guilt being a heavy black substance that everyone else can see that weighs me down. Anxiety riddles my body and I feel as though someone has stabbed me in the heart, I instantly want to fall to my knees and cry, what have I done? Before I can think on it any longer, Joyce is a welcome distraction, her smile beams around the church hallway as she rushes to embrace me. Can she see the guilt? Did she see me outside Sandra's? Is that the route she takes, where does she live?

"Thank you so much for all your help Faith, this is going to be a wonderful service and it's all thanks to you, I always tell your Mother, you're an excellent young woman of God, come on now we better get the kids all prepared." Those words are like my karma, for all of the perverted actions. A slap on the face to wake me and open my eyes to the reality and gravity of what I've done, I'm no longer an excellent young woman of God, I'm disgusting, full of sin and bound to be sent straight to hell.

The next few hours pass quickly with the presentation running smoothly. Church isn't as packed today with both weekends away which means there are less people for me to hide away from. I feel like if I speak to anyone they will know, they'll see straight through my deceit and into my tainted soul. The service is taken up mainly by the presentation and I don't have to listen to hatred being spewed. I can't shake the feeling that I'm painted in scarlet and that my cards are marked and the devil has stolen me away. Why would it feel so amazing if it was wrong?

At the end of the service as he always does, Pastor Leacher offers anyone who would like to be prayed for to come to the front of the church. My legs start to move me up before I give it any real thought. This is what I'm trained to do, I sinned, the devil is ruling my life and now I need God to take over. I need him to wash me clean again. I don't utter a word to Pastor Leacher. He asks God to put a hedge of protection around me and continue to shape me into the woman of Christ that he wills me to be. He moves onto the next "sinner" and I fall to my knees sobbing with my hands raised in the air. My vocal cords are silent but my inside I am screaming, yelling at the top of my voice for God to take it all away, make me normal, don't let me fall into the devil's trap. It's not abnormal for people to act like this in church and no one bats an eyelid which I guess is a good thing, I'd rather not answer any questions about why I'm a tearful mess. I don't stick around after the service even avoiding Joyce who I know would be looking to thank me again for all of my help. Shannon is busy chatting to some friends, probably telling them about Gavin as I slip out the front door and hurry to my car where I sit sobbing uncontrollably. I need her, she makes me feel safe and amazing but now I feel dirty and repulsive too, why can't this all just stop.

CHAPTER 23

I clean around the house, making sure it's in perfect order for my parents returning home, they're both very house proud and hate anything sitting out of place, it's all part of their image, makes them look like the perfect family. Looking at the bedsheets I slept in with Addison takes me on a rollercoaster of emotions, the overwhelming guilt and self-loathing along with the excitement and want for more. I just want to to see her again and to feel her touch. I wash the bedsheets and change my bed, this time opting for a white spread with bright pink blue and green flowers on it, it brightens up my room.

I don't have to hide anymore, at least not from everyone, so I give Addison a call and tell her about my morning, about how I've been crippled with guilt. Like always, she makes me feel better, telling me that I have to take it day by day and that there's no rush for me to come out, I just need to minimise the people I hurt along the way, for example Gregg. I know what she's getting at and I understand, I can't keep stringing him along. I explain that I'm not ready to come out yet but I know that I can't keep Gregg thinking we'll be together and I'll deal with that. Just talking to her on the phone puts me back in that whirlwind trance which helps me escape all bad feeling. We tell each other how we miss one another and end the call abruptly as my parents come walking through the door.

"I knew you'd have this house spotless Faith, didn't I tell you Liam?" Mum's smile is wide and I can tell that her weekend has been a much needed break from home life.

"Yes, that's my girl and I hear the service went really well this morning?" Dad wasn't even at church, how does he know this? He has a way of finding out everything, I think it's a part of his character, and it helps him to control everything in his life. It's almost like a few days ago he didn't hit me so hard I felt like my nose would come out the back of my head. I have to act happy families again. For how long will my Mum let this happen?

"Awk, yea Daddy it went so well, the kids loved it and Pastor Leacher seemed pleased too, all that hard work finally paid off." I try and act pleased to be speaking to him.

"That's good Faith, you're back to your old self." My Dad has a look of pride on his face, as if the smack he gave me has taught me a lesson and that's why the service went so well and I put the work in. Having something in my life he doesn't know about makes me feel good, even if it is a dirty secret.

Gregg stops by for Sunday lunch, the whole time I can't help but let my mind wander into paranoia, can he tell? I mean I have cheated on him? Will he smell her when he comes to my room? Will he know someone else has been kissing me? As he kisses me and holds me my mind is screaming for him to get off. I can't look him in the eye, I can't bring myself to touch him. He's not what I want, I know that, how am I ever going to tell him? Will it break his heart? He chats at the table to my Dad about their weekend away and they share memories. Mum begins talking about how the girls are planning another weekend away. That means money, which means my Dad will be bubbling behind the smile he's putting on for Gregg. I've mastered the art of changing the subject with my parents over the years, especially when I thought the subject could cause a massive row between them. I begin talking about the Charity Ball Shannon is in the final stages of preparing and how I'm going to town with her tomorrow to get a gown. Mum is excited too and says she's been looking forward to it for months. Mum loves all types of events they're her escape, anything to get her out of the house I suppose.

We finish lunch and head to church together all in my Dad's car. My mask has been perfected again, the perfect Christian girl with the perfect family and boyfriend. Gregg sits close to me in the back seat, rubbing my thigh affectionately. His touch is unwanted but I don't let it show, instead I reach down and hold his hand, he'll think I'm being sweet but really I just want her horribly large hands to stop touching my leg. I don't want anyone touching me, only Addison. She's mine. In my mind I'm hers. I feel like I'm betraying her now that I'm back with Gregg. I didn't feel so bad about betraying Gregg when I was with Addison. I'm starting to feel bitterness towards him, but I do care about him. Here goes my mind again.

CHAPTER 24

Mum is off to the gym for her Monday morning work-out, she doesn't go over the weekend, so Monday is always the toughest day, well so she tells me, I wouldn't know, I go to the gym once a month if I'm lucky when she drags me. I much prefer to put my headphones in and go for a run in the fresh air. Mum and Dad seemed happy this morning before he headed to work, which was nice to see although I know deep down that it never lasts long. I know that it's not going to last long when I finally tell them this week that Gregg and I are finished. I just need to pluck up the courage to tell Gregg first. I'll have to make up some story about why I'm not happy with him. When I chatted to Mum this morning I wanted so much to just pour out my heart and soul but I don't think she would ever accept me. She is so proud that I'm finishing University this week, she's always said I'll make an amazing teacher, my Mum inspires me, in some ways she's so strong for what she deals with but she's also weak for putting up with it.

When Shannon and I go shopping we're normally out all day, so I've opted for black skinny jeans, white converse and checkered black and red shirt, just something comfortable for what could turn out to be a very long day. My Mum would hate this outfit it's not girly enough for her, good job I started getting ready after she'd left for the gym. I'm eager today. Ready to go half an hour before Shannon is due to call in for me. Thank goodness Shannon doesn't need to get an outfit. I've told her that, she knows how I feel about going shopping when she needs an outfit.

I head downstairs making myself a strong coffee and sit in the bright conservatory, the sun beaming in through the countless windows. Gregg has text asking me to be his date to the ball. He's trying to be sweet, although I never really had a choice. I was always going with him. How can I break up with him this week? It's not fair, it'll ruin the night for him, his family, my family and then that will ruin it for Shannon. He wants me to tell him what colour dress I get, so he can get a matching tie, speaking to him even over text makes my insides wobble like jelly, but it's not excitement anymore, it's just disgust, guilt and dread.

"Hey beautiful," the novelty and sexiness of that New York accent seem like they'll never fade away as I answer the phone to Addison, I giggle nervously, my stomach going on another rollercoaster ride just with the sound of her voice. We talk constantly until she's starting her shift at Harmony. She tells me how Sandra is making her go to the ball and how she is dreading it, though she says she'll enjoy it more than I'm there all dressed up. I tell her about Gregg texting me and the playful mood of the conversation quickly changes. I grasp now how much this matters to her and so it should.

"I'm sorry Addison, I just can't do it this week, and it's not that I don't want to. I just don't want to ruin everything for everyone at the ball." I can hear Addison sigh down the phone.

"I understand Faith but it's just hard." I change the subject to me calling into see her today and that seems to suffice in cheering her up at the moment.

***

131

Shannon and I stand looking at one another with the biggest smiles we've ever had on any Monday.

"It's perfect Faith!" We've trawled around almost every shop in Belfast and Debenhams was our last stop, I felt defeated until now, I've chosen a sleeveless maroon floor length gown with laced pattern throughout it has a small slit up one leg, showing my tanned smooth leg. A little cleavage shows, not enough to make my Mum or Dad refuse to let me leave the house. The neck shoulder area is embellished with shiny diamond like stones.

"I love it." I beam my face blushing a little as a few other women in the changing room stop to look at me, no thanks to the sales assistant who is practically shouting over the shop that she's never seen it sit so well on someone. "That diamond jewellery set your Mum and Dad got you will just be amazing with that, won't it?

"I'll get the coffee you go grab us those seats while they're free." I tip my head towards the corner window seats that I love, it used to be for the view out the window but now it's because I can see the whole shop, meaning I have the perfect view of Addison. The young man standing behind the counter takes my order and says he'll bring the coffee over. I set two plates in front of Shannon one with a fifteen the other with a maltesers square.

"You take your pick I'm running to the bathroom." I see her eyes light up when she sees the buns and my words fall on deaf ears, I turn on my heels, heading up the stairs to the bathroom.

As I go to walk back down the stairs I spot Addison moving stock about in the upstairs storeroom, my face is immediately brighter and I smile from ear to ear. Her back is to me and I creep into the room checking no one is around and move up behind her grabbing her waist, she almost jumps out of her skin and pushes me playfully when she turns around.

"Well that was a pleasant surprise." With a level of authority she walks straight to the door, closing and locking it, before walking me with her hands on my hips back against the wall.

"I've missed you Faith, so much." I feel her soft moist lips meet mine and she sucks gently on my bottom lip, the feelings between us are almost visible as our kiss gets more heated. It feels like there's an explosion in my heart as she slides her tongue boldly inside my mouth, her hand slides up the front of my shirt and cups my boob, pawing at my bra. I moan into our kiss, my hands wandering up the sides of her tight fitting black shirt. Her tongue is now running slowly down my neck then I realise where I am and that Shannon is waiting.

"I'm sorry, I need to go back down to Shannon." My tone is obvious, I don't want to but I must, Addison lands another soft kiss on my lips and embraces me for a few seconds, her strong perfume intoxicating.

"I'll talk to you later babe."

I get to the bottom of the stairs and see Gregg sitting on the couch opposite Shannon, the only thing that stopped me vomiting was that I hadn't eaten today. What is he doing here? Probably on his lunch break, he has a right to a cup of coffee I guess and he is my boyfriend, I try to hide the disappointment on my face as I walk toward them both. The disappointment shows, when I realise Shannon has allowed Gregg to eat half of my Fifteen, I sigh, may as well finish it now. Shannon bores Gregg with details of the Charity Ball although he seems quite keen for a guy, he's glad I picked maroon and not a more girly colour and he's off to get his matching tie. I feel bad I was bad mouthing him in my mind for being here when he wasn't going to stay long anyway. I love Gregg, as a friend, not in the way that I should. I don't want to be with him at all. I feel awful for that. I watch as Addison clears up the table in front of us, she smiles over at us and everyone say hello. Gregg says his goodbyes and leans over kissing my lips.

"I love you Faith." He beams, his smile so wide it is childlike, does he have to do this right in her face. I can feel Addison's eyes burning on me, I need to speak.

"I love you." My words are dry and without real feeling, practically said as one syllable. Gregg doesn't notice but I can tell Addison does as she glares with her piercing blue eyes straight into mine, hurt showing on her face as she walks away.

***

I've skipped the Bible study tonight to focus on perfecting my final assignment, though most of the work is done, I just want to make sure that it's bulletproof. 10,000 is a lot to perfect. I've had so much on my mind, I'm glad I got it out of the way as soon as it was set. Otherwise I'd be screwed. It's strange, I feel a sense of achievement and for once, rather than accepting that God deserves the glory, I decide maybe for once, I'll take some credit for my hard work. It feels refreshing.

Addison and I have chatted on the phone for hours now. I couldn't even tell you what about, most of it completely random, like her telling me Canis Major the Great Dog constellation hosts the biggest star in the known Universe. She seems to know a lot of facts, I like that about her. Her intelligence isn't something she boasts about, it's something I figured out for myself, she's humble. Is there anything she's not? She just seems perfect. The way I see perfect has been completely redefined recently and to think I thought I was happy. It gets late and we yawn down the phone to each other, neither of us wanting to end the call.

"I wish I could have you here with me Faith." My smile is huge and I scrunch my nose up at how cute she is.

"I wish that too, I will be with you though, soon. I promise." She makes the softest most pleasant kiss noise down the phone at me.

"Goodnight honey."

Chapter 25

I'm standing out the front of Queen's University, an amazing building, a piece of history and a landmark for those living in Northern Ireland and those who come to visit our country. It's hard to believe that it's been 4 years since I first stepped foot in here. I'm almost expecting someone to roll out the red carpet and for a marching band to start playing. I get nothing of the sort apparently handing your final assignment in isn't as big a deal to everyone else as it is to yourself. At least this is my achievement and I haven't given God the credit for it, he didn't sit hours slaving or assignments or attend hundreds of classes.

I arrive home to Mum, Dad and Gregg all standing in the kitchen with 'Congratulations' banners and balloons, Mum has prepared a massive meal for everyone and they pop a bottle of champagne, non-alcoholic of course. Well it's not quite a red carpet and marching band but I appreciate the gesture and my blushing face and giant smile show that. Imagine I fail the last assignment. Well at least I'll have gotten a roast dinner out of it. I do love my food. There's a sense of excitement around the dinner table, it's strange. Perhaps handing in my last essay is as big a deal to everyone else, well at least my family and Gregg. Of course Addison is pleased for me too, she sent me a massive message telling me how proud she is and how she can't wait for us to celebrate together. I'll get to see her on Thursday for the Charity Ball, at least that's something. Knowing that she's proud of me is an immense feeling, everyone around the table has commented on God's work and how far he has brought me, honestly.

"Mum you do realise the Charity Ball is in a couple of nights? We'll be busting out of our dresses if we keep eating like this." Mum laughs but continues to scoff her creamy mashed potatoes. My Dad doesn't laugh, I think he's controlling over my Mum, he wants her to be slender, he said before if she put on weight he would leave her, I don't know how much jest there was in that comment. My Dad's must see himself as the picture perfect man. If only he was as nice on the inside as he perceives himself to be on the outside.

Dinner concludes and we all gather in the living room for a cup of tea, Dad puts on the God Channel, not exactly what I want to be watching but I don't have a choice. We watch an American preacher telling people to call up his healing line. He shares stories of others who have been healed. I wonder can they heal homosexuality. I mean if God can cure everything then surely it's possible. There goes that part of my brain that in still brainwashed with hate and bigotry, it's hard to shake. Of course God can't heal homosexuality because there is nothing to be healed.
"I was up so late last night, I think I'm gonna go to bed Gregg." I smile up at him almost sympathetically.
"That's okay. I'll finish watching this and see you tomorrow." I hope not I think into myself but try and keep my mask in full force.

***

I've text Addison to tell her about how those thoughts are creeping back into my head and haunting me at every given moment. She reassures me but it's harder when I'm not with her, I don't have the same sense of security. I wish so much she could just come and be with me, hold me and tell me it's all going to work out. Is it all going to work out? I begin to panic while I text her and this comes across. Her next message put my fears at bay for another day and almost brought a tear to my eye. No one has ever written me a poem, no one has ever invested enough emotion to do so and these words are powerful to me. I didn't even know she wrote poetry, I've told her about mine but generally I'll have to ask her questions to draw information out, it's of the things that draws me to her.

It's high time that you looked around,
Pick up that head of yours, stop looking down. Your dreams inside can surface now,
And if you can't walk into that dream somehow, Then I'll carry you to where you need to be.
I'll be your eyes when you cannot see, Your ear when the cries are all you hear, Your shoulder when no one else is near. By your side now and I won't ever go, It'll take time my friend for you to grow. You've got fight inside you, I can tell,
And if I have to, I'll carry you out of this hell. I will carry you.

Chapter 26

I've spent my morning making sure my tan is going to turn out perfect for tomorrow. Shannon is panicking because Gavin is coming with her. It's the first time he'll meet everyone, though they haven't told people they're an item yet, I'm pretty sure from what she is saying that they are. I'm so glad she's finding happiness, I look forward to meeting this Gavin to suss out if he's up to standard for my best friend, I would hate to see her get hurt. She doesn't deserve that, to calm her fears I tell her to come over to mine tonight, we'll share a small Chinese and watch a film. The Chinese has to be small otherwise my dress will be like Clingfilm on me.

I sit in the living room chatting to my Mum about looking for teaching jobs next year. Some of the older ones from church had to move to England to get teaching jobs as they're scarce over here. Mum doesn't want me moving away and I understand that, I'm her only daughter and I'd be leaving her with a monster of a husband.

"Mum, do ever wonder if maybe what we believe is wrong?" My Mum looks at me with a confused look.

"What do you mean?" I sit forward, hoping she'll open her mind.

"Well you know, our church says what's right and wrong and we believe them, what if they're wrong." My Mum shakes her head pouting at me.

"Faith, Pastor Leacher knows his scripture well enough that whatever he's telling us is straight from God's word." I know

I'm not going to get anywhere here. I was contemplating telling Mum about how I feel inside but today is not the day. I'll save this bombshell for another.

I've decided to use my energy elsewhere, somewhere it will be appreciated, Addison. When I wake in the mornings now I don't think about Gregg, I don't even send him a good morning text anymore. She's all I think about. I want to write her a poem like she did for me. I can imagine her reading it as she stands in work, her face will light up the entire shop. The feelings I have for her are almost indescribable but I'm sure I can get that across even a little bit.

Right from the start,
I knew you'd steal my heart. Your eyes saw past my face, Into my heart, that hidden place.
Your smile it spread from you to me, I knew that we were meant to be.
I fell fast for all that you are,

I'd found my own little sunflower.
You inspired me without even knowing,
More and more of your heart you were showing. You had so much love ready to give,
Now Without you I don't think I could live.

***

Shannon and I lie back on Mum's cold leather recliners but they're masked with the heat of my thick duck feather filled duvet covering us, we laugh hysterically at Bridesmaids which Shannon makes me watch at every given opportunity. We're stuffed full of Chinese takeaway and have just popped open two tubs of Ben & Jerry's cookie dough ice cream. The small Chinese turned into a full binge session and I am not genuinely worried that my dress won't fit. At least I won't have to go and play happy couples with Gregg.

"Here, Gregg was telling me about Sandra's niece, that's crazy she's allowed to keep working in Harmony even though she's a dyke." Shannon's words have pierced me somewhere deep inside. She's insulting Addison and if that isn't bad enough she's also insulting her best friend. She doesn't know though and I don't really feel she means any harm. It does make me wonder about all the times I stood and preached to gay people at the Gay Pride march, how belittling it must feel for someone to tell you you're going to hell because of love.

"I like Addison, I don't think it's fair for us to judge her Shannon." My best friend frowns at me, maybe she's jealous I've been spending time with Addison, I have thought about that but I've text her and she's always busy with Gavin. Shannon now appears to be spewing venom and the anger is clear in her voice, she feels passionately about this and normally when that happens she won't let it go.

"It's disgusting, God made Adam and Eve not Adam and Steve. Isn't that what they say?" she retorts.

"Yea I guess." I murmur. I just want her to stop speaking, I feel like I could erupt into hysterical crying.

"Well I think someone should say something? I mean Sandra needs to know how people feel, I don't wanna go in there with some lesbo staring at me." Shannon laughs brassily, her ignorance a shame and her disgust is evident. I'm ashamed that this how my best friend feels.

"I don't know Shannon, I wouldn't get involved. It's a bit dramatic to think she'd be staring at you. Anyway tell me about this new guy you've been texting, Gavin?"

Shannon is distracted chatting about Gavin, how he comes from a Christian family and does Christian youth work for his church. She goes on and on about him, the whole time I remain silent, I can't get her harsh words of my mind.

As our film ends Shannon hops of the sofa and gets her shoes and jacket on, she looks tired though I don't know what I'm talking about because definitely look tired too. I switch the TV off and Shannon gives me a squeeze.
"I'll see you tomorrow night. I cannot wait for you to meet Gavin. It's going to be amazing!"

***

I lie in bed, it's disgusting, 'I don't want some lesbo staring at me,' I can't get Shannon's words to leave me. Gregg tries calling me but I ignore him, he'll assume I'm sleeping and leave me alone I hope. How am I ever going to tell Shannon? Is she going to hate me, think that I stare at her? Everyone is going to think the same as her, how hard it must be for people to go through this, I know people go through it all the time because I looked it up online. People say it always gets better but I don't know how it can. I just keep thinking about a quote someone put on one of the Coming Out forums. 'Everything will be okay in the end if it's not okay then it's not the end.'

CHAPTER 27

It's the big day, the day of Shannon's much awaited Charity Ball. I'm looking forward to it, only because I'll get to see Addison. I don't care much for the rest of it, having to pretend I'm happy with Gregg and sit with my family pretending to be someone I'm not. I am looking forward to meeting Gavin though and I hope he's as nice as Shannon makes out. It's almost noon, I didn't sleep until late last night and thought I'd treat myself to a lie in. Mum is going to want to start getting ready soon, she'll do my hair and makeup and we'll spend a girly day together. I love days like that with Mum, I know I'll want to tell her how I feel inside but right now I just don't have the courage. I don't know if my Mum will accept me, knowing that breaks my heart.

I avoid Gregg's calls once again though I do text him, it would be rude not to. I tell him I'm busy getting ready and that I'll see him tonight, I just can't wait for tonight to be over. Though it also gives me a sense of dread, I know after tonight I have no more excuses, I have to break things off with Gregg. I'll then need to explain that to my family and I want to tell my Mum the truth. I refuse lunch, I feel as though if I eat I'll throw up everywhere. I can't wait to get to a point in time when I'm happy, when I have Addison but I have a life that doesn't consist of crying persistently every night. What a relief it will be when it's all over.

***

6pm and I stand waiting for Gregg to pick me up, I'm in the hallway pacing, I have my hair up in a sophisticated up style with some small curls hanging down, I guess having a Mum that looks after herself isn't so bad when you need your hair and makeup done. I've never had so much makeup on before but I feel good. I've been texting Addison on and off all day, I can't wait to see her all dressed up, I bet she'll look absolutely incredible. Every minute I'm not with her feels like an eternity. I just want her to be mine, really mine and she wants the same. I've never felt so compatible when anyone before, it's like we were made for each other. Gregg rings the doorbell; he's stood holding a single red rose, smiling like he's the happiest man in the world. I'd much prefer a white plastic rose from a rose seller in town. At least I could take it without feeling bad. This only makes me feel more guilt. I wish I could just tell him and get this over with. He kisses me on the lips, the touch of him. I don't want him kissing me. I feel like I could run away, I want to run away. We walk to the car arm in arm, looking like the perfect couple with the perfect life ahead of them. It's never been more apparent to me that looking at someone and making a judgement is so wrong. People are never as they appear, scratch the surface even slightly and you'll realise that everyone has skeletons in their closet.

The charity ball isn't turning out how I'd expected I'm stuck sitting at a table with my Mum and Dad, Gregg, Shannon, her parents and Gavin. I can't even see where Addison is, there's so many people here, about 200. I'm scared to text her in case Gregg sees me. Gavin is as lovely as Shannon, the way he looks at her, the way he treats her Mum and Dad with such respect, he seems like the perfect gentleman. I for one am totally aware though that he could be wearing a mask as part of this Christian masquerade ball I've found myself entangled in. For now though I'll give him the benefit of the doubt. Gregg keeps telling me how amazing I look, touching my thigh under the table, I hate him touching me. It makes me feel used, like I'm giving my body away to someone for nothing, when I don't really love them.

As we finish our meal Pastor Leacher takes to the stage to thank everyone for coming and gives a short speech on the importance of supporting missions in Africa. He speaks for around 10 minutes, though it feels like 10 minutes too long. His constant hatred of homosexuality gives me an inward bitterness towards him. If it wasn't for his sermons all of these years then maybe I wouldn't feel like I loathe myself. I wouldn't feel like a disgusting person inside, that I'd let the devil steal me away and that no matter how good of a person I am, when I die I'll go and burn in hell forever. As he closes in prayer, the DJ begins to play some upbeat chart music, carefully selected by Shannon, censored to ensure no offense is caused.

As people begin to mingle I finally spy Addison standing awkwardly beside Sandra who is chatting away to some old folks. Everyone around me is busy talking and I'm standing beside Gregg like a spare wheel. I take the plunge and decide to go over. I don't care if I'm leaving Gregg because to be honest, he is boring me. Addison is wearing a lilac ball gown. The type that doesn't look good on a hanger but when it's on the perfect body it looks amazing. It's on the perfect body, her hair hangs in loose curls and she's sporting more makeup than she usually does. Good grief, she is absolutely stunning. I'm aware of everyone in the room, I'm scared that she'll touch my arm or something in a way that will reveal our secret. She embraces me and it's like all my troubles are swept under the rug again. I breathe deeply, her perfume sending a rush through my body. I hold onto her for longer than I should with all of these people around. I feel like everyone is watching me, I don't know if I'm being paranoid or not.

Our conversation is interrupted when Pastor Leacher takes to the stage. He is joined by Gregg who is probably going to speak a few words on behalf of the youth fellowship who have visited the missions in Africa before. How many times are they going to get up and bore people this evening? Just let us get on with our night. All of our attention to turns to them and Pastor Leacher speaks for another few minutes, thanking various people for their helps and support.

"I'm not going to steal the show, so I'll hand you over to Gregg." I can see Gregg look down at me, he better not call me up there, he's done this before as if to say we're joint at the hip, I haven't been at the youth fellowship for weeks but yes he calls me up and I oblige. I look as Addison, letting out a sigh and she gives me arm as squeeze as I pass her.

I get to the stage and as I stand beside Gregg, looking at him with half a smile, though I'm sure he can tell by my face that I do not want to be on the stage. I feel like everyone looking up at me knows, they know my secret. Maybe Gregg knows and is going to reveal it to everyone in the room as punishment for my sin. My mind races as he turns to me, holding the microphone in his hand, and immediately drops to one knee, pulling out a black suede box and popping it open to show a sparkling diamond ring. I'm sure by now I am chalked white; I feel my mouth dry instantly. My heart has stopped, I'm sure of it. I feel like I'm about to fall off my feet. What is he doing? Please no!

"Faith, I want to spend the rest of my life with you, to have a family with you and to give our lives over to Jesus, You're the most amazing girl I've ever met and I love you more than anything, Marry me?" I feel as though Rhonda Rousey has landed a flying kick to my stomach as tears almost flood out of my eyes.

I've been staring down at him for way too long now, my face in my hands as I sob. How can I say no? What can I say? Everyone is watching, my family and his family. I try to catch a breath, swallowing hard to try and stop the flood of tears. I stare into Gregg's brown puppy dog eyes they're beginning to fill up with what could be tears of joy. My body begins to tremble, I need to speak. I need to say yes. I don't have a choice. I look down at the floor, Addison is stood staring at me with her hands clasped held up to her mouth, I can see the shock in her eyes. I can see the dread in her eyes. I know I want her, I know I need her. Help me, Addison, please help me. She's saving me, staring at her, it's giving me strength. I put my head down and run off the side of the stage and down the few steps that take me straight out the fire exit into the car park. I can hear the gasps from inside. I can hear the crackle through the speakers as the microphone drops to the floor.

Chapter 28

Gregg followed me, of course he did. I'm standing at my car. I have no keys, no bag, I need to leave and I don't want him near me.

"Faith, Faith please," his voice is trembling, he's sobbing, he's broken. It's like he's just dumped a tonne of guilt onto my shoulders, the tears stream like a river down my face, how am I supposed to tell him? I need to tell him now. I want to scream it out.

"Gregg, I'm sorry, I'm so sorry." I have my back against me car, he walks closer to me, placing his hands on my sides.

"Please don't Gregg, I can't do this anymore." I place my hand on his chest and move him back off me, he steps back.

"What have I done? What has happened?" I can't look at him, I'm ashamed.

"It isn't you, it's me. We're not right for each other." I shake my head, wiping the tears from my face.

"What has changed? We've been so happy, you're killing me here." I don't want to tell him, do I need to tell him?

"I haven't even told my family Gregg, I don't want them to know, I can't tell you, I'm sorry, please just know that I'm sorry."

Gregg isn't going to let this go. I need someone to bring my keys, where is my Mum? Where is Addison? Is everyone giving us space, thinking we'll walk through the door hand in hand with a ring on my finger like I've just had stage fright? "We don't have to get married Faith, if it's too much, if you're not ready then I understand." He is pleading with me. I can't

handle this anymore I just want the ground to swallow me up.
"It isn't getting married, it's me and I just can't be with you
anymore." I can see the confusion on Gregg's face, this isn't
fair on him. He's getting irritated.
"Tell me what it is Faith!" His voice is loud and startles me,
making me sob more.
"I'm gay Gregg." I hang my head, holding it in my hands.
"What?" He knows what I said and he lets out a shocked
laugh. I look up at him, I have to face him and show him that
this is real.

Why has she come now? No. This isn't right. Gregg is crying
his eyes out, like someone has just ripped his heart out and
stamped all over it. "Sorry, I was just bringing your things."
Addison hands me my bag.
"I'll go back inside." Her voice soothes me, I don't want her
to leave. Gregg stares at her, the rage evident in his eyes.

"Her, it's her isn't it? She's got inside your head." He points at
her, spitting as he speaks. "You're sick. You're messed up wee
girl, you're disgusting." He begins spewing venom at Addison,
what has she done to deserve this? "Leave her alone Gregg,
this isn't anybody's fault, it's me, it's who I am and it can't be
changed." His head shakes in disbelief. "You've been seeing
her? Behind my back are
you kidding me? Wait until your Dad hears this, I can't believe
you're doing this to me, to them?" I gasp as he speaks. The
hatred is building in his eyes.
"Please don't tell my Dad Gregg, please, I'm sorry, I'm so
sorry."

Gregg storms straight to his car and drives off, revving his
engine loudly and speeding out of the car park, what have I

done to him? I need to leave, I need away from here, I can't have anyone else seeing me, asking me.

"Can we go, please?" I turn to Addison taking my bag off her.

"Of course we can." We get in the car, I don't know where I'm going but I need to get far away from here, I feel like I want to drive off a cliff. Make it all end, make this hurt end. I'm hurting so many people.

"I'm sorry that happened to you Faith, like that." I try to hold back my tears as I drive, I can't even speak. My brain has barely registered what has just happened.

I pull in at the side of the road after driving aimlessly for a few minutes, I bury my head in my hands leaning on the steering wheel, sobbing. "I can't do it, I just want to run away." I hear Addison unbuckle her seatbelt. She runs her hand up my back, resting in on my shoulder, giving it a squeeze.

"I know right now it feels like you have one million reasons to run but let me be the one reason you stay." With that Addison wraps her arms around me, pulling me close to her. Just like that, momentarily, I'm in my safe place, I've found my Saviour.

I finally find my last piece of strength that Addison has given me, wiping my face free from tears, my makeup must be an absolute mess, not that I care right now. My phone is buzzing constantly in my bag. I need to answer. I need my Mum to know I'm okay. I lift it out, there are 30 missed calls, from my Mum, Shannon and Gregg. I only want my Mum.

"Faith baby are you okay? Tell me you're okay?" My Mum's voice is quiet and worried, she sounds like she's been weeping.

"I'm okay Mum, I just can't be with him, I'm sorry, I didn't know what to do, I'm sorry." My Mum is breathing heavily down the phone. "Sweetie, come home and we can talk?" I swallow hard I can't go home, not tonight. "Mum, I'll come home in the morning, I just need space, I'm sorry." Addison reaches over, supportively holding my hand.

"Where are you going to stay? How do I know you're okay?" The anxiety is evident with every word.

"I'll be okay, I promise, I'm staying with my friend, I have to go, I love you Mum." I hear my Mum sniffle she must be upset this is breaking my heart.

"I love you too Faith, stay safe, please."

***

We call by both of our houses, sprinting upstairs to only grab clothes for tomorrow, worries that my parents or Sandra could arrive back at any minute but we escape in time. Addison has found us a room to stay in, no expense spared as we walk into the Europa Hotel.

"You know there was probably cheaper ones Addison?" I try and joke, though my lungs seem incapable of laughter.

"Only the best deserve the best." She smiles sweetly though she looks drained like me. This whole situation is bound to be taking its toll on her too. I fixed my makeup in the car a little, though I'm pretty sure I still look like I've been dragged through a bush.

"Check in please, Addison Preston." Even her name is sexy, the way she says her name is sexy. She's my distraction, when I'm with her it's like I can see a light at the end of the miserable tunnel I'm running through. She places her arm over my shoulder, pulling me in for a squeeze as the lady behind the desk gets our keys sorted, I expect the woman to look up in disgust but she doesn't. Maybe she thinks two girls who are in love are normal.

"Room number 276, enjoy girls." She smiles brightly.

"I'm ordering wine. This night needs to end with wine." Addison says exhausted as we walk into the hotel room. It's amazing, massive, with beautiful décor, various shades of red, complimented with a luxurious king size bed. I've never been in such a rich hotel.

"Do you fancy anything? You look like you could do with a drink." Addison jokes as she picks up the room phone, "I don't mind, I think I would try anything to make me feel better." I throw myself onto the bed, staring at the ceiling.

"I'll make you feel better, don't worry about that." She purrs, winking at me, her jokes make me laugh. Even after such a horrendous day and the weight of knowing what I face tomorrow, she can still make me smile and laugh.

She lays in the bed beside me, lifting her arm for me to come into her and I oblige immediately, she lies on her back and I wrap my body around hers, my head resting on her chest. She kisses my head softly.

"I'm so proud of you Faith, you done something tonight that proves you are a lot stronger than you think, everything is going to be okay, I promise." I squeeze her even tighter now.

"I couldn't have ever done this without you, I would have been stuck, living a lie, I owe you my life." Addison continues to land soft kisses on head as she caresses my side with her hand. "You don't owe me babe, I owe you, for making me the happiest girl in the world. This is your achievement, you are such an incredible girl, never forget that." She wraps her arms around

me, holding me close to her, breathing me in. Her touch still gives me goosebumps. I want to stay in these loving arms forever. Why can't I just stay here forever?

***

The hotel room a window that overlooks bars and restaurants in Belfast, there are two comfortable red chairs and small table, Addison ushers the room service in, and they leave the drinks on the table. Really, three bottles of wine? This girl must be dying for a drink. We both take our seats.

"Well this isn't how I expected this night to end." I force a laugh as she pours two glasses of wine. "You know what they say unexpected nights are always the best." She hands me a glass of wine. Without even thinking I take a swig of the pinkish liquid in the glass and screw my face up almost instantly.

"That doesn't taste too good." I laugh as I see her smile widening at my screwed up face. "Yea, I'm just thinking you'll never have had wine before. You don't have to drink it sweetheart." Her pet names make me blush.

"No, I think I'll just grin and bear it, maybe it'll take the edge of this crazy night."

As I sit talking with Addison, I feel so lost in the moment, like someone has plucked me out of Belfast and set me down in some foreign mystical land. Addison tells me how relieved she is that she can have me for herself. I feel my cheeks redden and wonder when that will stop, when will she stop making me feel so nervous? Do I really want it to stop? I can feel my face begin to heat anyway and I think it might be the wine. No one has ever told me about wines secret heating agents before but I'm pretty certain on my theory. I tell Addison I'm going to tell my Mum tomorrow and she says she can tell Sandra. I fret about whether or not my Dad will let me stay in their house, how will I survive without them? I won't even have money to live. Addison tells me that I don't need to worry, I could stay at Sandra's and she can help me out with money until I'm on my feet, she says she's inherited a lot from her Mum. She has an answer for everything and she can always make everything better.

***

The wine has most definitely got to my head, I've suddenly gained confidence, I'm never confident, this feels weird. Addison speaks to me about how she wants a dog and I am really enjoying listening to her but I've been dying to kiss her all night, I need to kiss her. I stand up, walking over to her, smiling widely, still looking down at times as nerves try to creep back in. She sits back in her seat, looking me up and down, the burning of her eyes is almost enough to strip my confidence away but it's too late for that, I sit myself down on her knee, my legs hanging over the side of hers.

"Hello." She says playfully, as she rubs her hand up my thigh. I lean in, landing a soft kiss on her lips, though it doesn't stay soft for too long as we begin to kiss more passionately than ever before. Is it the wine? Maybe it's because I'm finally hers.

Addison stands me up, walks me over to the bed and pushes me down on it, she's being quite rough, like she can't wait any longer. I land on the soft cushioned bed.

"I really want to rip that dress off you." I can see the hunger, the passion in hers eyes. Her words send serious heat between my thighs, how can she do that with just a few words.

"In fact, come here." She pulls me backup of the bed. Where is she taking me? My heart pounds quickly in my chest as she leads me to the massive wet room. The shower is huge, more than enough room for the two of us and this is what Addison has in mind, this will be weird, I've never showered with anyone before.

Addison turns me around, unzipping my dress at the back, slowly sliding it off my shoulders as she kisses my back softly, running her warm hot tongue over my skin.

"I'm gonna fuck you so good Faith." She bites on my shoulder, making me gasp. Her words turn me on so much, now I want to rip her dress off. She unhooks my black laced bra and slides my thong off, letting it fall to the floor. I'm completely naked, right in front of her. I don't even want to try and cover up, the bathroom is very dimly lit and the way she looks at my body, it's like she adores me, it makes me feel like a supermodel. I turn around and face her, then twist her body, unzipping her dress and following the same pattern as she did. I need to learn off someone. I'm anxious as I kiss her shoulders and this is apparent with my rapid breaths. I struggle to unhook her purple bra, it makes me blush and I hear her giggle a little. She's wearing purple lace knickers, I want to pull them off with my teeth, I could never do that. She has the most incredible bum, so round and firm. I let her knickers fall to the floor as I admire her amazing body.

Addison steps into the shower, adjusting the heat to the perfect temperature before taking my hand and pulling me in, the hot water on my body make me feel such a relief. She begins to kiss me softly, her moist lips meeting mine with intention as she slides her tongue into my mouth. Her hand runs up my back to my head as she pulls me more into her kiss, I can feel her excitement as she plays with my tongue. I don't even notice her stepping me backwards but I can now feel my body pressed up against the tiled wall, the hot water still streaming over our bodies. I feel so dominated, like she's in control though I like her in control, I could never be as confident as her. She slides her hands down my sides, caressing my body, her touch and the hot water is causing me to moan into our kiss.

She takes my hand from her side and moves it onto her exposed breast, so firm and pert, they're perfect and her nipple hardens under my touch. I play with her nipples, moving them in between my fingers, and she begins to do the same to me, I hope she's not mimicking me because I don't know what I'm doing. Addison moves her lips onto my neck. I raise my head, the water beating off my face only making me want her more. She bites down on my neck, making my body push forward into hers. I feel her hand on mine over her breast as she slides it down her body, I feel as though I could faint. She wants me to touch her there. I don't know what to do? How do I make her feel like she makes me feel?

Addison moves her face off my neck, stepping back a little. She stares into my eyes, making me feel unbelievably wet as she slides my hand further down, her hand on top of mine. My hand slides her bare sex as she moans out.
"I want you to make me cum Faith." Hearing her say those words almost makes me come and she moves my hand up and down her slit, almost teasing herself. Then all of a sudden I'm on my own, she's moved her hand back to my body, straight to my wet hot sex. She slides her hand up and down, making my knees bend in pleasure. Then slides one finger inside my warm slit, I moan out her name and slide my finger in, hoping she'll feel the same immense feeling that I do. I didn't think she could look any more amazing than she usually does, but

here now in the shower her body soaked and dripping, her hands on my body and my hands on hers, she looks like an absolute Goddess.

She moves her finger to my clit, circling it teasingly and I do the same, it's like she's teaching me and I must be doing something right because she's biting down on her bottom lip and her knees are bending at times too. I can feel my body wanting to give into her already as she places more pressure on my clit. I do the same, hearing her moan because of my touch is enough to make my heart shutter. There's so much feeling between us, so much passion, you can almost see it. The hot water dripping on my body, the steam it's so hard to keep on my feet and to concentrate of rubbing her clit with more pressure as she does the same to me. She leans her face into me her breath heating my lips.

"I want to fuck you so bad Faith." I moan out as she slides a finger deep and hard inside me. I wasn't expecting that, I try and continue to pleasure her but I can't possibly she slams her finger inside me again. As she moves closer to me she places my hands above my head with her free hand. She doesn't want me to keep touching her. She wants all my attention to be on how she is making me feel. She begins kissing and biting my nipple, as her finger finds a slow and sensual rhythm moving in and out of my tight sex. My moans become louder, I try and keep them in, I don't want whoever is next door to hear, how embarrassing.

Addison takes her free hand and covers my mouth. This sets my whole insides on fire, the sexiest thing anyone has ever done, it has to be. She stares in my eyes, smiling at me as she moves her finger inside me, touching whatever it is she touches in there that makes me weak at the knees. Removing her hand from my mouth she kisses me hard and dirty. Her tongue exploring every inch of my mouth as she begins to slide two fingers inside me, hard and fast, leaning against my body to keep me on my feet. I scream out in pleasure, I feel my body begin to reach climax. Addison falls to her knees, continuing to move her fingers inside me.

"I want you to come on my face." She lands a hard lick on my clit, my body presses down on her tongue as I scream out louder than before. She licks harder while fingering my sex with two of her slender fingers. I feel my body jolt, up and down, her tongue still persisting. My heart is about to explode and I can barely catch a breath as my body gives into her. I cum hard and the feeling is unbelievable. I've never felt anything like it before. She slides her fingers out of me and plants her mouth onto me, sucking and kissing, making my body wriggle back and forward until I can't handle anymore and have to pull her face away.

"You taste so good Faith."

CHAPTER 29

I open my eyes, giving a small yawn I'm laid on my back and Addison her head on my chest, I look down lovingly at her, kissing her head softly. I don't feel good this morning and my guesses are it's the wine, in fact I feel could throw up. Oh no, is this what a hangover is like? I move Addison off me, trying not to wake her but have to jump off the bed and run to the bathroom, completely naked, I don't feel so confident in the light of day or when I'm leaning over the toilet bowl throwing up.

"Are you alright?" Addison's concerned voice is closer than I'd like it to be as her hand rubs up my back.

"Did someone have too much wine last night?" she jokes as I feel my body wretch forward. I nod my head, disappointed in myself. I feel like the entire contents of my stomach have now been flushed away as I take a sip of water from the glass the hotel staff have kindly left beside the sink, almost as if they saw me coming.

"I need to get home Addison, I'm sorry, I don't want to leave but I need to see my Mum." I have no idea what time it is, it could be noon or 7am. I just know I went to bed last night feeling like I'd won the lottery. I can't even remember falling asleep in Addison's arms but she practically had to carry me in from the shower as my legs were like jelly.

"Don't be sorry honey, you can always call to mine tonight, or call me if you need to talk, it'll be okay though, please don't be scared." Addison reassures me. I search for my phone, my battery is dead, great my Mum has probably been trying to call me and she'll be worried sick. The alarm clock beside the bed tells me it's 8am. That's good she may still be in bed.

"I'll be okay I just need to tell them the truth. I'm their only daughter, they have to understand." I do have doubts in my head but like with everything, I feel if I say it out loud that it'll become more real.

I pull on my Navy Jack Wills sweats and Maroon jacket to match, topped off with my maroon converse. I pull my hair back into a messy bun before washing my face under the cold tap. I stare at myself in the mirror, how did my life get to this place? How could I feel so amazing last night but so down in the dumps today? I just need to get this over with, I need to call Gregg later too and see if he will let me explain any further. I don't want him to think that it's him or that this is personal. I shake my head, letting out a deep sigh, then she comes up behind me, wrapping her arms around me, like that, everything seems a million times better. It's like I feel like I'm losing myself, losing my mind and then my Saviour reels me back in.

***

I drop Addison off at Sandra's house, embracing her like I'll never embrace her again, holding her with all my might in a huge bear hug. Then we share a soft kiss but not just any old kiss, it was the perfect kiss. All of her kisses are perfect. "I'll give you a text as soon as I get my phone charged, thanks for everything." Addison smiles as she gets out of the car, I can't help but stare at her behind in her tight blue jeans.

"Okay, you know everything is going to be okay, I promise, just be yourself." I smile, though on the inside I am crying. My heart feels weak. I feel weak, I don't know that I can do this, I feel like driving and not stopping until I'm so far away that nobody even knows my name. Then I remember what Addison said to me, I have a million reasons to run but she is my one reason for staying.

My Mum's car is parked at the front of the house and I can only pray that my Dad's isn't round the back. He would normally be left for work at this time. Though I'll just have to wait and tell my Mum if he's home, I need to tell her first. I think she'll be more accepting, she'll understand more. She has to, she's my Mum and I need her more now than ever. I feel like I could throw up again as I close the front door quietly behind me. I hear the TV in the living room is on, anxiety is tearing through my whole body and I'm almost shaking. I walk into the living room. My Dad is standing as if he's about to leave and my Mum is sitting on the couch with her back to me. My Dad sees me first, his icy eyes cut through any hope I had of a peaceful morning with Mum, his face crimson with anger.

I'm lying on what feels like a camp bed, there's noise but I can't hear what it is properly. There's a ringing in my ears, what is this? I pull my eyes open it takes so much strength. The rest of my body feels numb like someone has injected me. I see a strange face staring down into my eyes. "Faith, we're on our way to hospital, everything's okay. We just need to get you checked over." What how did this happen? The last thing I remember is my Dad coming towards me, for a split second I thought he was going to hug me, my heart melted, then he lifted his hand, now this. I'm in an ambulance, though the sirens aren't on, it can't be that bad. I'm frightened, I begin to panic what about my Mum, where is she, has he hurt her. "Mummy" I scream loudly.

"Mummy," like a child who has fallen and hurt their knee. I feel a squeeze on my hand. "Don't worry baby I'm here," my Mum sobs.

We arrive at the hospital and I'm not beginning to feel serious pain, my face is throbbing. I can't begin to imagine how bad this is. What about Addison. I need to tell her I'm here. They wheel me into a room and move me so I'm sitting on what feels like a kitchen chair, still, my whole body feels numb, I reach my hand up to touch my face, checking that I exist, it doesn't feel like it right now. I pull my hand away, the pain, it's unbearable, I try to cry out but begin to choke on what tastes like blood. The Doctor comes over, standing in front of me, he places one of things they take your blood pressure with on my arm, is there any need for this? Then after he's checked his results he listens to my heart rate. I think this is a bit extreme. Just plaster me up and let me go. The Doctor asks me to hold something to my face, I agree, though why can't he do this himself? I think he wants to take me out of the daze I'm in, I'm starting to feel dizzy. I'm holding what is now a blood soaked bandage against the right hand side of my face. The last thing I remember was my Dad coming towards me, tears fall from my eyes as I realise what's happened and I look at my Mum who is sitting on a seat a few feet away from me, with tears in her eyes and her head in her hands, she looks broken.

I know now just how hard my Dad hit me, hard enough that my flesh is torn from my bottom lip, all the way to my chin, hanging open and seeping blood. The Doctor explains this to me in a lot of description which is great. He says I've hit my head but they've been able to staple it on the way to the hospital, he wants to do a quick x-ray after just in case. A policeman has just walked into the room and asked to speak to my Mum, she gets up immediately still sobbing. My ability to hear or speak has left me, I can see the Doctor's lips moving, and behind him my Mum stands in hysterics. I feel a small prick to the side of my face which I assume will numb the pain. I wonder if the Doctor could inject whatever that is into my brain and heart just to let me breathe again. I don't know how many stitches the Doctor is forcing into my swollen face and I don't care either, I just don't care anymore. My face feels like it does after I've had work done at the Dentist, that's where I am right now, lying back on the Dentist's chair, none of this is real.

The Doctor finishes working on my face, he can see that seeing my Mum talking to the police is distressing me, he walks over and closes the door.

"Okay Faith, I want you to have a wee lie down on this bed now okay?" I nod my head, as I stand up I see my face in the mirror, the doctor failed to mention that my full face is swollen like Jose Aldo after 13 seconds with Conor McGregor. I begin to panic I'm scared, tears stream down my face.

"Okay Faith, let's lie you down." The Doctor takes me by the arm, clearly not wanting me to look at my face any longer. I don't know if my Mum called the police or if they just come when someone gets attacked? Has my Dad been arrested? I don't want that.

"Okay Faith, whilst your Mother is out of the room, I need to ask you a few questions we're going to need give you an X-ray for your head, is there any chance that you could be pregnant?" He acts like this is a completely normal question. I frown as he stands looking cool as a cucumber. "What do you mean?" I ask confused.

"Is there any way that you could be pregnant?" I almost choke on my own saliva. Is he completely kidding me right now? I'm lying here looking

Quasimodo and he's asking if I might be pregnant. I spent last night being fingered by a woman and he's asking me this? Then my mind darts back, that night with Gregg, I didn't do anything to stop it happening? There is no way. "I've had sex but it was just once, probably over a month ago." Speaking is a treacherous task and the skin on my face throbs. The Doctor nods and smiles gently.

"Please don't say this in front of my Mum." He understands, I can tell, he does this all the time. "That's okay Faith, I'll need you to take a wee test for me before we send you for an X-ray alright?" I nod. My eyes begin to fill up though I know the chances of me actually being pregnant are slim to none. Is my period late? It's irregular anyway. I have no idea.

The Doctor tells me he wants me to rest on the bed for bit and that the nurses will be in to check on me. I lift my hand to my face, as soon as my fingers touch it a burning sensation ripples through my body. I hear the door open behind me, my Mum rushes over, holding my hand, like she's been waiting to have me alone, her eyes are red and puffy from crying and I can see her eye is swollen.

"Mummy, did he hit you?" I ask through gritted teeth, trying not to allow my face move at all.

Mum nods, she's in floods of tears, there really isn't anything as heartbreaking as seeing your own Mother cry.

"Gregg came by late last night, he told us." She chokes as if she's still trying to process what she's been told.

"I'm sorry Mum, I'm sorry." Mum holds my hand tightly.

"Faith sweetie, you have nothing to be sorry for. You're my daughter. I'll always love you no matter what." Mum swallows hard, looking into my eyes.

"The police are going to want to speak to you Faith, I had to call them, I had to, look what he's done to my girl." She wails, it's like after all these years her eyes have finally opened, if seeing me like this is what it finally takes to make her walk away then my cuts and bruises are worth it.

***

I stretch my body out on the hard but now warmer bed, a small white blanket placed over me. Mum is still at my side clutching my hand, rubbing it gently. I must have fallen asleep, I feel exhausted like my body has been through the wars and the Doctor has been drugged up on serious pain killers, though they are working.

"Mum, I need to speak to Addison." I watch my Mum's face there isn't the disgust that I'd expected.

"My battery is dead do you have your phone?" I half expect my Mum to go off on one, scream and shout and maybe finish off the job that my monster of a Dad started.

"Yes, I'll text Sandra and get her number for you? Or do you know it?" I try and force a smile but my face aches.

"I don't have it, text Sandra please." Mum gets her phone out and happily obliges.

"I'm so sorry Faith, I tried to stop him, I tried but the police have him now." Mum gives me her phone.

"There's the number, do you want a few minutes? I'll go get a coffee or something?" My Mum is being as accommodating as possible, I'm shocked to my core. I hope this isn't just because I'm hurt, I hope that she does still love me. The paranoia makes me think that everyone will hate me.

"Thanks Mummy, you don't have to be sorry, you didn't do this, we're going to be okay, I promise." She smiles down at me, nodding her head in agreement then gives my hand a final squeeze before wiping her tears away, slipping on her strong woman mask.

Addison answers the phone, it's clear she has no idea what's happened, I thought maybe word would have spread to Sandra if my Dad had been arrested.

"Hey baby, are you okay?" Hearing her voice makes me weep, I need her. I want her here with me.

"Addison I don't want you to panic." Immediately she panics, it's clear from my voice that I'm panicking too. I'm forcing words out through a closed mouth.

"What is it Faith? Are you okay? Tell me?" I'm ashamed and embarrassed of my Dad, to think that he feels this way about me all because I'm in love.

"I'm at the Mater hospital Addison, my Dad attacked me, I'm okay though, they just have to check me." She gasps loudly down the phone. "What? When? I'm coming now, Sandra can take me. I'm leaving now. Are you okay?" I knew she would freak out, I would too.

"I'm okay, come to A&E, they will bring you to me, Sandra can come in, she could speak to my Mum. She's not in a good way." Maybe speaking to Sandra will make my Mum see the gravity of the situation, it'll maybe make her leave for good, I still have doubts that she'll go back to him. I can hear Addison begin to cry now and it's too much I can't handle hearing it.

"I have to go, I'll see you soon." I sob.

***

I hear my Mum outside the room of the small door, she's talking and it sounds like she's trying to explain what's happened. The door swings open and Addison rushes in, she's in flood of tears, I've never seen her be anything but strong before. When she sees my face her jaw almost hit the floor and she almost screams out in shock. She grabs my hand holding it tight, her chest is rising and falling rapidly like she's in a blind panic.

"I'm okay, I'm okay." Sandra and my Mum stand behind Addison, Sandra putting her arm around my Mum's shoulder to comfort her. My Mum gives me a nod, Sandra gives me a sympathetic smile and they leave the room, allowing me to see Addison alone.

"Listen, I need to tell you something, please don't say." Addison doesn't look like she can handle another bombshell. I need to tell her, I can't deceive her or keep anything from her.

"I don't even think it's possible, when Mum was out of the room the Doctor said he wants me to take a pregnancy test before my X-ray." Her face falls into her hands, she's in shock, I wouldn't blame her for running out of the room and never looking back, this is supposed to be our honeymoon period.

"Faith, I promise, everything will be okay, you need to believe that, no matter what we will be okay," she squeezes my hand gently. The Doctor enters the room.

"Would you like to step outside for a moment?" he smiles at Addison and she goes to leave.

"No, she's okay." I struggle.

"Okay Faith, there's a wee toilet in there, he points to a door facing the bed, I need you to try and get me some pee in this

167

wee cup, okay?" I nod, sitting forward on the bed, I feel like I could have whiplash, my back and neck are so sore, like I've been flung about. I don't remember much of the actual attack. Maybe my memory will come back in time. I struggle to pull myself off the bed Addison helps me up by the arm and walks me over the door.

***

I don't even think my brain has really processed what's going on, I feel like I've been here for hours, I thought I'd really slept but it turns out I haven't and we haven't been here long at all, less than one hour. The Doctor was keen to test my urine and I just about got a sample for him. He told me not to stress out and that he'll be back shortly. All three of them are now in the room, looking down at me with pity. They all look so solemn, almost like they're looking at a corpse. They're not speaking much either. Addison continues holding my hand, my Mum gave her shoulder a squeeze at one point, it warmed my heart. Maybe I was wrong about my Mum all along, maybe she won't hate me and I won't have ruined her life. The door knocks and my Mum steps outside and reappears within a minute or so.

"Faith sweetie, the police want to speak to you and take a few photographs, is that okay or will I tell them to come back later?" Mum's voice is soft, she sounds frightened, and I'm not surprised.

"That's okay, you and Sandra go and get coffee sure, and Addison can stay with me."

Addison takes a step back as two PSNI officers enter the small white room. I use the wee remote to adjust my position so that I'm sitting up more. There is one male officer probably around my Dad's age early 50's and one younger female officer who looks a bit pale. Perhaps she's never seen a face like mine before.

"We'd like to take a short statement from you Faith, are you okay to answer a few questions?" I nod, my mouth drying up, I'm frightened, are they going to lock my Dad up? Is that really what I want? The female officer begins.

"Okay Faith, I just need you to talk me through what happened today?" I look at Addison, wanting a bit of reassurance, just seeing her face makes me feel safer and I feel more at ease to speak.

"I stayed with Addison last night, when I got home this morning, Mum and Dad were in the living room, I just remember him coming towards me, his hand raised and then I don't know, I can't remember." I become upset and tears start to stream, Addison steps forward, clutching my hand.

"You're okay Faith." The police woman tries her best to not sound persistent, I know my account was short but I don't remember.

"Okay and did anything happen before this?" My mind races, should I spill about the years of abuse?

"For years, he's hit me and my Mum though more my Mum lately. He found out I was gay last night, he didn't like it, that's why it happened." I become more tearful.

"I'm just going to take some photographs, then we'll leave you, we have your Dad in custody and have charged him with grievous bodily harm but we can explain this further later, you're safe now, is that okay?" The policeman finally speaks, he probably has a daughter my age, probably thinking my Dad is a monster and he is, but he is still my Dad.

The familiar Doctor enters the room, he doesn't seem old

enough to be a Doctor, he's pleasant though and that more than I can say about my GP who I avoid visiting at any cost.

"Okay Faith, do you want your friend to stay here?" He asks, looking at Addison.

"Yes, she's okay." He nods his head, looking down at my stomach at least I feel he is anyway. "I'm going to want to run some tests Faith, you are pregnant." That ringing in my ears floods back, I feel Addison grip my hand so tightly it almost hurts. The Doctor's lips are still moving but I'm not hearing a single word. This can't be real.

CHAPTER 30

Addison hasn't left my side all day she's telling me that no matter what she's never going to leave me. I feel like my brain has been mashed, like some sort of side to a Sunday dinner. I'm pregnant. There is life growing inside me. My X-Ray showed that the swelling was nothing to worry about, I got lucky. I told my Mum I couldn't go back home, she agreed to move some of my clothes to Sandra's. Sandra says I can stay for as long as I like. It's her and Addison in a 4 bedroom house. I assume as a Christian she wouldn't want us staying in the same bed. While they were away the Doctor listened to my belly, Addison and I heard a heartbeat. This all feels so surreal. What a difference 24 hours can make.

"We're not going to need to keep you in Faith, but we will need to see you again soon, you can phone for an appointment on Monday okay?" I nod at the Doctor and I'm sure by this point he probably thinks I'm a mute who is incapable of stringing a few words together. If I knew where my life was headed or what my future held for me then I'd be a bit more in tune but I am the definition of confused right now.

"Mum, what about Dad? Where is he?" I put my head down, looking as the floor as I gather myself to leave.
"Darling, the police will be keeping him in custody and he'll go to court on Monday, they might bail him then." I swallow hard, how can I do this to my own Dad? I can't think about it right now. I need to get out of here.

The car journey to Sandra's drags, she drives so slowly and the whole time I wanted to scream for her to put the foot down. Amazing Grace played softly in the background and I put my head back, resting my eyes, wondering if someone was going to wake me up and tell me this was all just a nightmare. Unfortunately that wasn't the case, we arrived at Sandra's and Mum and Sandra sat downstairs having coffee, while Addison helped me get me stuff in. I've got a small room next door to Addison it's a typical spare room with white and cream bed covers though at least I have a double bed. There's a nice rosy smell, probably coming from the potpourri which is strategically placed on the nightstand beside my bed. I have white floral wallpaper which doesn't look it's been changed since the 80's but I'm not complaining.

***

I can still hear Mum and Sandra downstairs, chatting away, though their tone in quite low and I think my Mum has probably been coming clean about all the years of abuse she's been subjected to. I'm sure it feels like a million breezeblocks have been crane lifted off her weak shoulders, Mum never talks to her friends about real life, it's normally just church and God. I don't even know where Addison is and I know it's awful but right now I don't feel like I care. I've been sleeping on and off for a few hours, my duvet is placed carefully over my head. I just want to hide away from everyone and everything I don't want any of this to be real. My tears are a reminder that though I've managed to let one secret loose, I now have another, potentially more massive secret to unveil. Not only am I gay and in love with Addison, I'm now pregnant with my ex boyfriend's baby. I don't want a baby and

I don't want his baby.

"Sweetie, are you awake?" Addison's soothing voice reminds me of how much I really do care. In moments of hardship I guess it's easy to forget to be grateful for what we have, there are always people worse off. This is true. I pull the duvet off my face Addison is sitting on edge of the bed, how long has she been there for? It's dark outside and there's a small lamp on the nightstand which dimly lights the room.

"I'm awake." I smile as she reaches for my hand squeezing it. She is so stunning, inside and out, it's like I can see right through to her soul.

"It's 10pm those painkillers are probably making you sleepy. Can I get you something to eat?" I shake my head, the thought of eating, I don't even know if my jaw could muster up the strength right now to chew.

"Is my Mum okay?" I ask, wondering if Addison has been downstairs with her and how my Mum is handling being around her.

"Yes Faith, she's getting there, she told me she just wants you to be happy and if I make you happy then I better stick around." She giggles sweetly.

"Awk I can't believe how well she is taking all of this how am I ever going to tell her about it Addison?" Addison doesn't need to ask what I'm talking about, she just knows.

"You don't need to worry about that tonight Faith, I want you to relax, I'm going to bring you some toast, I'll see if Sandra has any straws for some tea." She leans over, landing a soft peck on my forehead, for a split second I am at ease.

CHAPTER 32

It's early evening, Sandra and Addison are at the table having their dinner and I'm sat in the living room waiting for Gregg to arrive. I feel like someone has let a thousand spiders inside my body, they're crawling around my head and insides, making me want to jump out of my own skin. Gregg has been trying to call me, I feel like I owe it to him to speak to him face to face and tell him we're expected a baby. I know he will want me to keep it. I know his family will too. I wish I could just make it go away and not tell him but I don't feel I could live with the guilt. My Mum urged me that this was the right thing to do, Auntie Orla needed her at the house to help with packing and I was glad, I couldn't look at my Mum's broken face anymore. Seeing what I've done to her rips my heart apart. I just hope that one good thing can come from all this and that's my Mum finally leaving her abusive marriage, part of me still doubts that this will last long.

A car pulls up outside, my stomach is in knots. This is my mess, it's my fault and I have to clear it up. I open the door as Gregg walks up path, he doesn't look like he's slept much either. I have an overwhelming urge to run at him and slap him for telling my Dad before I did? Was it always going to end up like this? It isn't Gregg's fault, I suppose I'm just looking for someone to blame, I can only blame myself. Gregg gives me a hug, though I make no attempt to hug him back, feeling his arms around me repulses me, I hate everything physical about him. He can sense my disdain as he moves himself off me, I show him through to the living room.

We're sat facing each other, I opted to sit on the lone chair, I knew if I sat here he couldn't be beside me, couldn't make any attempt to touch me again. He's wearing a rugby tracksuit, navy and red, though I know he hasn't been training, maybe he needs comfort. His face could do with a shave, it's like everyone involved is wearing their heartache on their face. I would hate to hear what other people think of my face if this is what I'm thinking about theirs.

"I'm sorry Faith I shouldn't have told your Dad like that, I didn't know this would happen." Gregg's tone in sombre.

"That's fine it's not your fault." I try to force half a smile out but I can't. The tension between us in unbearable, he's looking at me, so lovingly, like he's longing for me. It reminds me of how I look at Addison, I've never looked at Gregg like that and I never will. I need to just tell him, I half expect him to fall on the floor screaming, and then tell me it'll all be okay that he wants our baby.

"Look Gregg there's something we need to talk about." He nods as I speak.

"I know Faith, I miss you so much, I know this is all in your head and you'll snap out of it, I know you love me." In the name of Christ, is he actually serious? What do I need to do, carve the words lesbian into my forehead in order for him to understand?

"No Gregg, we're over for good. I'm with Addison now. I'm sorry for hurting you." I breathe deeply, I know I'm hurting him and I do have empathy but I can't continue living a lie and pleasing people. I need to be honest, for the sake of everyone else and myself. Gregg is staring at me, his eyes filling up, I hate seeing a man cry. "Faith you don't mean that, she's inside your head, you don't mean that." He's shaking his head, he's confused, I don't blame him, so am I. "You're wrong Gregg Addison makes me happy I'm in love with her." I have to be blunt I need this to sink in. He puts his head in his hands, his face red with anger, it's like a switch in his mind has flicked.

"If that's the case and you're actually staying with that dyke, why have you trailed me over here?" His voice is loud and aggressive, a side to him I haven't often seen.

"I'm pregnant Gregg." The silence in air is almost visible, like a dark steamy element that takes away his ability to speak.

"What?" The shock is apparent; I'll have to tell him ten times like I had to with Mum.

Gregg is now stood up pacing up and down the living room, towering over me as I sit and sob on the chair.

"How is this possible? Why would you not take a pill? What have you done? You're a stupid bitch." His words are harsh and he means it, I wasn't expecting this. Like it's my fault, like I wanted this to happen. I didn't get pregnant on my own, I often wonder why when women have abortions they are blamed as if it was solely them choosing this. Men need to take some responsibility as well.

"Gregg that doesn't matter now, we can't change it." He stops dead on the floor, glaring down at me.

"Yes we can, you're not having my child, you're not bringing my child up while you're mentally ill, are you crazy? You need an abortion. I'll pay for it, you're not bringing my child up while you're with that dirty lesbo it'll be as fucked up in the head as you. You're having an abortion. Do you understand?"

I've almost gone into a trance, I'm hearing his loud screams but I'm not processing them, I can't. I can't handle it. He's so hateful, why is he so hateful? He wants me to abort our child?

Perfect Gregg, the perfect boyfriend, is now showing his true colours. If only his Dad could hear what his perfect son is spewing. Sandra rushes into the living room, even a man of Gregg's stature would fear Sandra she's like a wee pit bull.

"Time to go son," she takes him by the arm and walks him towards the door. He turns, looking at me disgusted. Addison is stood in the hallway, watching as what resembles an episode of Eastenders unfolds. Before I even realise what's happened Sandra pushes Gregg out the door, slamming it and pushing Addison back. Addison wipes her face with her sleeve and tries to open the door as Sandra shouts at her to stop. Gregg the one my best friend said was a keeper, whose parents think has the sun shining out of his ass has just spat in Addison's face.

I jump off the couch, screaming obscenities at Gregg, though it's no use as I hear his car door slam shut. "How dare he? I'm getting onto his Dad." Sandra marches into the kitchen, she's going to phone Pastor Leacher, which means she's going to tell him everything, I'd rather she do it than me.

"I'm so sorry, are you okay?" I follow Addison as she walks into the kitchen, washing her face under the tap and drying it off.

"Yea I'm okay."How could I have shared so many years with this person? When put under pressure he's worse than the people he sits in church and judges.

"I don't care if he's your son Pastor, the boys a disgrace he needs a good seeing to." Sandra is screeching down the phone, she is furious. I can only hear mumbles when Pastor Leacher is speaking, I can't work out what he's saying but he sounds angry, Gregg must have spoken to him already.

"Is that right? You're supposed to be a man of God, what's it you quote when you condemn abortion? He knitted us together in our Mother's womb? Here you are a man of God telling this wee girl she needs to kill her child, you're a horrible man and our Addison will make Faith happier than your son ever could." Sandra slams her phone on the table, taking a seat. Her hands are trembling with rage, nobody ever stands up to the Pastor like that but Sandra doesn't fit the bill for someone who keeps quiet.

"Faith you're not to listen to any of them, that's your wee baby and you show them that you don't need them, I'm going to cover Addison's shift in Harmony today, you girls phone me if you need anything." With that Sandra shakes herself off and marches out the door.

"I've done so much to damage to so many people, this is a mess, my life is over," I sob as I sit at the kitchen table, unable to look at Addison who is sitting facing me. She reaches over the table, holding my hand.

"Faith it's going to be okay, you're not the first person this has happened to and you won't be the last, this happens every day, it's normal." Addison's words immediately anger me and I pull my hand away from her. Right now I don't care how many people this happens to, I care about those closest to me that I'm ripping apart. My upset turns to fury in an instant.

"I doesn't happy every day over here, maybe it happens every day in your world but in my world it doesn't, stop saying that it's normal, your normal isn't my normal." I begin to raise my voice.

"Faith you're talking nonsense, define normal? No one has died you need to calm down it'll all be okay." Addison speaks calmly now but firmly.

"No, it won't work it'll be okay for you you'll keep living your perfect life, while mine falls apart. Two women bringing up a baby is not normal!" I bow my head, my body jerks as I cry hysterically.

"I have far from the perfect life, don't dare speak to me like that, you sound like Gregg or your Dad! Waken up!" Addison snaps, how dare she. "Maybe my Dad and Gregg are right maybe you are inside my head, maybe it's all your fault, it wouldn't have happened if I'd never met you." I yell back, my temper breaking.

"All I've done is support you and you're throwing it in my face, if this is how you really feel then just fucking leave." She's upset, screaming at me, I stare straight at her, tears flooding from my eyes.

"I wish I'd never met you, you've ruined me, ruined my life."

***

I've ended up in the local park, walking aimlessly around, passing people who stare at my battered face with sympathetic and judgemental expressions. I keep my head down, I don't know where I'm going and I don't care, I couldn't stay in that house a minute longer, I'm sure Addison wanted me to leave anyway. Why am I blaming her, it's not fair but part of me believes if she never came along then I'd still be with Gregg living my perfect life. I've lost it all, my family hate me. I finally relent and answer the phone to Shannon, she's been calling me all day and she deserves to know the truth, she must know about my Dad, I bet the whole street knows. I need to be honest, I need a friend, someone who understands and will help me, tell me what I should do because right now my mind is an absolute minefield.

Shannon pulls up in the car park and I cautiously enter her car, embarrassed and ashamed of my face which is a reflection of my life right now. Shannon clips out her seat belt and reaches over hugging me tightly I knew I could depend on Shannon.

"I'm lost Shannon, I'm so lost." I cry into her shoulder, she releases me.

"Faith, come on, I know you, you're stronger than this, you can get through anything, I'm always going to be here." I try and smile but my face refuses to engage.

"Shannon, I'm pregnant, I'm in love with a woman, my Dad is in jail, what has happened to my life?" I bury my head in my hands, catching a glimpse of Shannon, her jaw is almost on the floor of the car and I can see why. I'm an absolute mess, I've done this myself and this is my comeuppance for letting the devil into my life. I feel a supportive hand squeeze my shoulder,

"Faith this is going to be okay, we can fix this, I'll help you." Shannon's voice is low and she doesn't sound herself, she's probably as confused as me. How can this possibly be fixed?

I finally manage to stop the tears though I know it'll be temporary.

"Faith you know, you can still put all this right, you and Gregg can be happy God will help you both through this." I look into the eyes of my best friend who is thinking God can fix everything, it's all she knows and I can't hold it against her.

"I can't Shannon, it's not like that, I don't love Gregg." Shannon shakes her head; I can tell she's judging me, why does she have to judge me?

"You don't have to be with Gregg, you can bring the wee baby up yourself, and everyone will help you." She just doesn't understand I don't know why I thought she ever would.

"I don't want to be on my own Shannon, I want to be with

Addison, I'm in love with her." If disgust had a face it would be staring at me right now.

"I knew she'd get into your head Faith, that's what those people do, she's manipulated you, it's not right, it's not fair." I swallow hard, begging her silently to understand, empathise and just support me.

"I know you think you love her Faith but if you stay away from her you'll realise, you need to stop seeing her, she's so sick and twisted." My heart breaks hearing her speaking about Addison like she's dirt on the ground.

Shannon won't stop talking, she's ranting, believing that she has all of this sussed out, she thinks that Addison has basically cast some sort of evil into my life and that I'm confused and need to be prayed for. What is wrong with her? Is she so brainwashed that she can't see true love when it's right in front of her.

"Shannon can you please stop, it wasn't like that, do you think I want to feel like this? Do you think I want to have to live like this? I wish I could be with Gregg, my life would be so much easier." Shannon stares ahead she isn't one who likes confrontation.

"Well you can be with Gregg, you're choosing to walk away, he's broken, he loves you, God planned for you two to be together and the devil is coming into your life and he will steal kill and destroy, you know that?" I can't listen to this any longer; the only person trying to get inside my head right now is Shannon.

"Can you stop speaking about Addison like she's evil, I love her she makes me happy how can that be wrong?" My voice is breaking and my body trembling, the upset and anger are eating me up and I feel like I could explode.

"You don't love her Faith, you're not in your right mind,

please open your eyes! Bad company corrupts good habits!" It's like she's eaten a Bible for lunch, the scriptures are flowing. "Shannon I tried so hard to fight this off, that's why I had sex with Gregg to try and make myself want to be with him, I can't change who I am." I feel a lump in my throat, the tears are making their way to my eyes, I don't want to cry anymore, I've had enough, I can't handle it anymore.

"I need to go." I slam Shannon's door shut and begin to walk again. The bitter air meets my face and the tears take this as an invite to start flowing again.

CHAPTER 33

I journey along the path nearing Sandra's front door, not too long ago I was walking up here to visit Addison and I was full of excitement and joy, I couldn't feel more different now. I can't get rid of my anxiety, everything that I once held so dear is gone and right now I don't have anything. I push the door open and walk coyly into the living room. Addison is sat in the lone chair watching some cooking program on TV, though she looks disengaged and doesn't greet me with her usual bright smile.

"Can we talk?" I sit on the couch facing her, swallowing hard. I don't even know what it is I want to say.

"What about?" she snaps back barely taking her eyes off the TV screen, all of a sudden she's interested in it.

"I don't want to fight with you and I'm sorry that I you were upset by what I said." I feel her eyes burning on mine.

"You don't know how much it hurts me when you say this is my fault, like I'm some sort of a disease." Her eyes are filling and her smooth skin blushes.

I breathe deeply, I just want Addison to understand how it feels to be trapped inside a life that isn't right for you, to lose everything and everyone and not know what's around the corner. Her life seems so perfect. I don't believe she knows what this feels like.

"I know and I'm sorry, I'm just trying to make you understand how I feel, this is tearing me apart and I feel so alone, until you lose everything and everyone I don't think you could understand." Addison takes a long deep breath and shakes her head as I speak.

"You think you're the only person in the world that's ever been hurt Faith?" Rather than making me feel happy and safe Addison is making anger build up in me, the type of anger I never want to feel towards her. I love her so much but she just doesn't get it.

"That's not what I'm saying, I'm saying you're happy, you have a good life! You're not riddled with anxiety all day and crying yourself to sleep at night wondering if you'd be better dead." I retort, why can't she just understand?

"No Faith, I'm riddled with self loathing all day believing that I wasn't good enough for my Dad to ever want to see me and I'm just crying myself to sleep at night with the last image I have of my Mum sprawled out on her bed, covered in vomit and stone cold dead from a pills overdose, that's what I deal with, I don't take it out on you or other people, I don't dwell in self pity and I certainly don't blame other people!"

I barely have time to process what Addison has just said, she storms out of the room, tears flowing from her eyes as she slams the door behind her. The bang of the door wakes me from my pity party and I'm realising just how selfish I've been. I had no idea that's what happened to Addison's Mum, she never told me and I never asked. I can't even begin to imagine what she's been going through alone? I'm screaming at her about her life being perfect and about how mine isn't worth living. What have I done? I've never seen her cry or get upset before. I place my head in my hands, drying my tears, I need to be strong, I need to be strong for her. I hear her bedroom door close, I can't leave her alone but it doesn't sound like she wants me near her, why would she? I've really upset her, I feel awful and overwhelmed with guilt but I'm used to that. I need to stop thinking about myself 24-7 and neglecting the people that matter, I've barely been in touch with my Mum, I don't even know how she's coping and any conversation I have with Addison is centred on my life.

I knock Addison's bedroom door softly, she doesn't respond. I can't just leave her it doesn't feel right not when she's in such a bad way. I open the door slowly Addison is sitting on the floor, her back pressed against the bed and her head in her hands. She is sobbing loudly I immediately begin to cry with her.

"I'm sorry, I'm so sorry." Addison doesn't lift her head, I sit beside her and pull her close to me and she clings to me, completely broken. For the past few weeks Addison has been holding me together, all the while she has been falling apart herself.

"I know none of this is your fault and I'm sorry I said those things, I'm so sorry. I love you." I kiss the top of Addison's head, the smell of her fresh scent filling my lungs. I'm overwhelmed with emotion the amount of love I feel towards her is crazy I never imagined love could feel like this, I now know what true love is.

"I'm sorry too Faith, I love you." Addison looks up at me, her eyes red and swollen from crying. "Don't be sorry, we're going to be okay, I promise." I kiss her forehead softly and hold her close to me. Usually it's Addison promising me everything will be okay.

We lie on top of the bed, Addison's head rests on my chest, she holds onto me like she never wants to let me go. I rub her temple softly, feeling my t-shirt wet under her tearful eyes, I try and be strong for her, reassuring her. I know she doesn't want to talk about it, not yet anyway, she just needs me to be here and I will. Her sobs penetrate my heart, every tear hurting me to the very core. I hold her tightly.

"I promise you everything is going to be okay, I'll always be here." I try and comfort her though it's difficult, nothing in the world will ever bring her Mum back, and nothing will take away the pain she is suffering right now. I can only be here.

CHAPTER 34

Waking up next to Addison is something I could used to, I would never get tired of it, not even if I woke up next to her every day for the rest of my life. We're on our sides facing each other, she's wrapped up and still sleeping, her breath heavy, she looks exhausted. I can barely remember last night. I have vague memories of changing into pyjamas and quickly dozing off again with Addison in my arms. I stroke her warm soft face, she presses against my touch with her eyes still shut. Her room is decorated with soft pastel colours, light greens and purples, which match her white bed sheets. The decor is quite cold, though it just makes being tucked up warm in bed with Addison even more enjoyable. Addison opens her eyes, screwing them up slightly as the light beams in from the open blinds.

"I love you." She leans in kissing my lips softly. The first words from her mouth this morning renew my strength.

"I love you too beautiful." I kiss her back, wrapping my arms around her.

We finally emerge into the kitchen after what can only be described as the best morning of my life. I've been craving Addison's touch and longing for her, this morning she showed me exactly why I'd been craving her. She gives my body so much attention, kisses every inch of it and makes me feel like a supermodel. Though it was hard to keep the noise down but that just made it all the more exciting. We've opted for similar dress this morning with our black skinny jeans and oversized t-shirts, though Addison definitely wears them better.

"Good morning ladies," Sandra beams.

"Do you fancy a wee cuppa tea?" I smile and accept the offer. Sandra is one of the most genuine loving people I've ever met, she's given Addison today off to spend with me which I appreciate. I've started today much better than yesterday, though I know that it's going to be a hard day for Mum and I, Dad is going to court and a judge will decide if he's allowed out on bail which Mum said is very likely. We don't even know what time, Mum said the police will call her and let her know. I've been trying not to think about my Dad, when I do I feel guilty and I know I shouldn't, this isn't my fault.

I sip over my tea as the three of us sit around the table waiting for my Mum to arrive, I hope she's been doing okay at Aunt Orla's, I know she would be well looked after. My phone buzzes and I glance down at the screen it's Gregg, again. He has been calling me non-stop from last night, texting me, begging me to speak to him. I don't know what I can do, I can't make this any easier for him if I could I would. I feel as though I owe it to him to speak to him but would I be betraying Addison if I did? I don't know, it's something I want to talk to my Mum about, I'm hoping she will have the answers. I silence the call and continue on with the small talk we're making around the table. It's as though we're all blocking out entirely the last few days and talking about insignificant subjects like the weather, though it is refreshing. Addison has started talking about how the people over here are so much different than the people in New York she says there is more of a sense of community. We all agree that this has good and bad aspects, it's nice to know there is support but it can also backfire when everyone knows your business and gets involved. It makes me think about how I must be the talk of my Street and also the church, though I don't care much to be honest, that's the least of my worries. I can't take my eyes of Addison as she smiles and laughs, I know that behind it all is a lost little girl, though she wears her happy go lucky mask so well.

***

Sandra and Addison have stayed in the kitchen and given Mum and I some privacy in the living room. My Mum looks more like her usual self today she's wearing smart black trousers and a white blazer, with a pink chevron top and matching high shoes. Her hair is sitting perfect and her makeup is over the top but that's standard for my Mum.

"Faith sweetie, the police called me before I got here, your Dad has been released on bail, I have a solicitor on the case, I'm asking that your Dad not be allowed near the house, if they agree then we can go back there, you and me, we can't be here there and everywhere." The thought of going back to that house fills me with a sense of dread however I know that my Mum and I should be entitled to stay there, the house is owned by them both, my Dad caused this, he shouldn't be allowed to continue on as normal while we suffer.

"I hope they can do that Mum, I don't like being apart from you." Knowing my Dad could be just around the corner forces my stomach into knots, I don't believe he would ever come around here but I didn't believe he'd ever hospitalise me either. I tell my Mum all about Gregg and Shannon, it's hard talking to my Mum and being open and honest about how I feel about Addison but I have to be, part of me still feels ashamed to talk about being gay but Mum doesn't act like it's out of the norm which is a pleasant surprise.

"He won't stop phoning me Mum, do you think I should go and see him? I feel awful and maybe now he'll have calmed down?" I'm confused yet again, I wish sometimes there was someone on my shoulder just telling me what I should do and when I should do it, maybe then life would be a little bit easier.

"You know Faith, Gregg is shocked and he's acting out because he's hurt, maybe talking to him calmly and just explaining everything, maybe it'll help." I feel like my Mum is giving me good advice, I don't know how Addison will feel about it but I don't want to hurt Gregg more than I already have.

"Okay, I'll see if he'll meet me later, I just want this all to go away Mum, I want to feel normal again." My Mum wraps her arms around me. "Everything is going to okay, I'm here for you, you have Addison and she loves you, even though you're incredibly sad, I can see you're in love and believe me that counts for a lot in life." I rest in my Mum's arms, returning briefly to my childhood, when I was hurt or upset my Mum would hold me and make up silly songs using my name, they always cheered me up, I've always been a Mummy's girl.

Sandra knocks softly on the door before walking in.

"Do you two want another wee cuppa tea?" I laugh at Sandra.

"You remind me of Mrs Doyle, always offering tea." We laugh together.

"No I'm okay, I must run on here, Orla is treating me to lunch today," my Mum gives me another firm hug.

"You call me if you need anything Faith." She then hugs Sandra and Addison before leaving, it must be church folk they love a good hug, though I think we all need it.

"I'm going to go and chat to Gregg today, I know after yesterday he probably doesn't deserve it but I feel like I need to." I look down at the floor, expecting some form of judgement from Sandra or Addison.

"That's understandable, just be careful," that American accent is still as sexy as ever and distracts me once again from the dire reality of my life.

"I will be, don't worry about me." Almost like he was listening, Gregg begins calling my phone. "I better get this," I walk out of the room and into the kitchen. Gregg sounds surprised when I answer the phone to him, I barely let him speak, instead I interrupt his apologies to tell him we can meet and talk but that nothing will be changing. He agrees but begs me to meet him in an hour and I relent, the sooner it's over with the better.

I stand staring out the kitchen window, there's a small sparrow hopping about the grass, it pecks below for a while before flying off, so free. I wish I felt that free, like I wasn't being weighed down by a thousand problems I don't know how to fix. I feel Addison's soft arms wrap around my waist, she kisses the back of my neck softly and rests her head on my shoulder.

"You know Faith, we should get a holiday, I think that's what we both need." The thought of escaping with Addison, somewhere far away makes my heart skip a beat, the only thing that worries me is that I might not ever want to return.

"I would love a holiday with you, where though?" I lean my body back against Addison, it's like she's become my Saviour again, she trails me away from my dark thoughts and makes me think positively about the future, our future. "Maybe somewhere hot with cocktails and white sands." I can hear Addison smile as she speaks. "We can look them up later, it sounds perfect I'll go anywhere as long as it's with you."

***

The feeling I have driving over to Gregg's house is a far cry from the excitement and joy I felt wrapped in Addison's arms talking about our dream holiday. I stand at the front door, taking in deep breaths and trying to calm my anxiety, what am I even doing here? I'm contemplating turning around and driving away when Gregg opens the door. His eyes are shifty and he doesn't look like he's had any sleep. He stands back allowing me to come in, I feel so terrible for putting him through this how am I ever going to make this right? I walk into the living room and take a seat on a chair, choosing my seat wisely again, knowing that Gregg can't get close to me.

"Do you want a drink or anything?" Gregg asks as he looks down at me.

"No I'm okay, I can't stay long." I speak lowly, looking into his tired brown eyes. He looks like a puppy, the same day it gets taken from its Mother, sad and defeated.

"I don't want to have an abortion Gregg, it's not right, I can't," Gregg takes a seat on the couch across from me, he sits forward, his eyes burning on me, he nods as I speak.

"I don't want that either Faith, of course I don't. That's my wee baby in there, a life that we created together, I want to be with you every step of the way." I can't cope, why is he still saying things like this?

"Of course I want you to be part of our lives but we can't be together, that isn't going to happen again." He shakes his head as if what I'm saying is farce.

"Shannon told me you wished you could be with me and you can, we can forget all of this." Those brown eyes are now filling with tears, it's devastating to see him like this, why would Shannon tell him that? She's supposed to be my friend and she has taken that completely out of context.

"That's not what I said Shannon should never have told you that." He takes a deep breath as I speak.

"She told me because she's worried about you, she knows we should be together and she knows Addison has got inside your head but that deep down you want to be with me, you just don't know how to break away from Addison, you don't have to go back there, you can stay here." I stand up, the anger and frustration building inside me.

"No Gregg, just stop, we're over, I'm with Addison and I love her!"

I've not shouted at Gregg much before or even raised my voice, through the years we never really had cause to argue, I never really spoke my mind, just allowed him to make decisions on my behalf. As I turn to walk away Gregg stands and grabs my wrist aggressively spinning me around to face him.

"You need to stop this, I won't let you have my baby and stay with her." I look up at Gregg his face is red with anger and his once loving eyes now look void, I try and pull my wrist away from his grasp but my efforts are in vain, I'm weak and no match for him.

"I won't let you, I won't let you bring this shame on me." Gregg yells at me, I feel his saliva land on my face as he spits his words out. I feel like someone has dumped a tonne of anxiety into my body, I'm so frightened I've almost frozen still. I can't find words I can't even process a thought. I feel my wrist released from his grip, without thinking I turn on my heels and run out the door, slamming it behind me. My whole body trembles as I start my car and take off in a panic.

I need to get home, well not home I need to get to Sandra's. I need Addison, I feel like I'm broken again, Gregg has scared me so much, filled me with anxiety, I thought he was going to hit me, I think he was, I don't know what stopped him. I've never seen him like that before. I just want to be held, to hear her tell me everything's okay to be okay. I pull into Sandra's street, there's a Police Car I don't know if it's at her house. As I pull up outside, an ambulance pulls up behind me. I sit still in the car, what's going on, two paramedics hop out of the Ambulance and walk up the path, Sandra is stood at the door in a state. My heart has almost stopped, Addison, what has happened to her?

CHAPTER 35

As I run up Sandra's garden path I feel like Olympic athlete Usain Bolt in the last 10 metres of his 100m sprint, adrenaline is rushing through my body and I feel sweat beating off my forehead, mixing with my tears. Sandra doesn't even have a chance to speak I rush past her and follow the paramedics into the kitchen. She's slumped on the kitchen chair, blood soaked into her hair, her face battered. I almost vomit at the sight. I cry out, trying to run to her but a policeman holds me back.

"It isn't as bad as it looks sweetie," my Mum whimpers as the paramedics inspect the wound on her face.

"Mum what happened?" I sob. Addison is beside my Mum, holding her hand tightly. She has my Mum's blood on her and she's chalk white like she's just seen a ghost.

"It was your Dad I never should have gone over there." My Mum sounds broken all over again. I cry hysterically, the sight of my Mum like this is just too much to handle, Sandra puts her arm around me.

"Come on into the living room. Give those guys some space love." I allow her to lead me out of the room.

I lean back on the sofa, staring straight ahead, trying to process thoughts, I want to kill my Dad I hate him so much.

"Why did he do this Sandra? Why?" Sandra is pacing up and down the living room, trying to compose herself.

"Your Mum went to speak to him, to ask him to leave the house, she said he tried to make her stay and when she went to leave he attacked her, she ran here, poor soul." She wipes a tear from her cheek and looks into the kitchen.

"You know it's not as bad as it looks love, they said the wounds are superficial, they're just producing a lot of blood, the police have him in custody, I hope they lock him up and throw away the key." Sandra's voice trembles, I feel like I've brought her into the middle of my now dramatic life as well as Addison, I've caused all of this. He could have killed my Mum I can't believe she went there to him. I can't believe any of this is real I'm never bringing a baby into this mess. I can't. I can't do it. The thought of having a life inside me sends a chill down my spine, I lean forward vomit spewing over Sandra's thick cream rug.

As Sandra rushes around the living room cleaning up the entire contents of my stomach, I'm in a complete daze. I feel responsible for what has happened to my Mum. This could have been so much worse, he could have killed her, I can't get that thought out of my head. My Mum walks into the living room, her head is bandaged and her blonde hair soaked with blood, she's swollen and looks like something off a Domestic abuse charity on the TV. I stand and hold her crying into her chest.

"You're okay my love, we're okay." My Mum is trembling, the paramedics are making their way out of the house, I heard her refusing to go to the hospital but I'm so numb I can't even speak to insist she goes. How has my life got to this point? I know Addison says that this happens every day but it doesn't make it any easier.

Auntie Orla has just arrived at the house and she's taken my place, holding my Mum. She is furious. She says they'll lock my Dad up now until he gets sentenced it's a relief to know he can't harm us anymore, at least for now. I just want to go home with my Mum I don't want to stay here anymore. I don't want anything, only to be alone to try and process the crazy situation I'm in all because I fell in love with a girl. Addison sits next to me on the couch and holds my hand, I'm sure she's reassuring me and I'm hearing her but I'm not really listening. It's a comfort to have her with me but I just want space and time. I can't tell her this I don't want to hurt her feelings. I don't want her to feel like I'm pushing her away. Am I pushing her away? Do I want to push her away? Not having a clear mind is something that I've faced more in the last few months than in my entire life, people say they're confused but they don't really mean it. I'm surrounded by so many people but right now I couldn't feel more alone.

Mum and I decide it's best if we go back to our own home tonight, safe in the knowledge that Dad is locked up. I can tell my Mum is missing home. I would do anything right now just to give her the slightest bit of comfort. Addison offers to come with me but I politely decline. I feel guilty for that and I'm sure she's wondering what is going on in my head as I can barely look at her or hold a conversation but it isn't just her, it's everyone. Sandra offers to cook us some dinner and bring it round but Mum and I know we won't be having a nice sit down meal together tonight. Instead we'll probably go home and cry together over the absolute state of our lives right now. Addison's words ring true with me now though, no one has died this could be a whole lot worse. I hug her tightly and tell her I love her before leaving to make the short journey home.

I make Mum and I a cup of tea in the kitchen and Mum sits looking out over the lights of Belfast in her sunroom.
"I'm sorry that I've caused this Mum." I fight back tears knowing that I have to be strong for the both of us.

"You didn't cause this Faith, he caused this, please don't blame yourself sweetie." Mum's voice is quiet, she isn't herself and I wouldn't expect her to be right now either. I join her on the couch and sip over my tea, she looks into my eyes and tries to force out a small smile.

"I just want you to be happy Faith, sometimes I wonder if this is a phase or you're confused." I swallow hard, I knew my Mum had taken this all too well so far and I guess this is to be expected. "It's not Mum, I know who I am I'm in love." My Mum nods as I speak.

"As long as you're happy Faith, I will love you no matter what just make sure that this is what you want." I take a gulp of my tea, in Belfast everyone always says 'There's nothing a good cup of tea won't fix.' I've just had a good cup of tea and I'm far from fixed.

"I know Mum, I'm sorry I couldn't tell you before, I was scared." My Mum reaches over placing a gentle hand on mine. "Don't be sorry darling, you know I did think about this, about you and whether or not you liked boys, many years ago but I was scared too and I didn't say anything, I'm sorry." I reach over squeezing my Mum tight. Knowing that she thought about this before and didn't tell me doesn't upset me, quite the opposite actually, it's like all of my thoughts and feelings have been validated.

CHAPTER 36

There's a certain silence that features only in a home without children. A silence that allows you time to reflect back on life, reflect over the weeks, months and years that have so fleetingly passed us by. It's a silence that I love. I'm sat looking over Belfast from my Mum's sun room the sky is so bright blue and clear. The only sound is my Mum flicking through the pages of a book at the kitchen table. My Mind wanders back to the day I snapped and took control of my life, that day that he and I don't like to say his name really hurt my Mum. I haven't spoken his name from that day and others know not to say it around me. He's where he belongs, stuck in a cell somewhere and when the time comes I hope they choose to keep him locked away for a long time. Regardless, he is nothing to me, just someone I used to know, and someone who used to control me. My Mum doesn't miss him she's a different person now. Completely free, she enjoys weekends away with my Auntie Orla, takes religion as a personal thing and doesn't go to church. I'll never get over the shock of walking into the house a few months back, Mum and Orla were sat at the kitchen table after too many bottles of wine, singing to Abba. I've never laughed so hard.

I have a perfect view of Shannon's back garden from here I always have a nosey in when I'm here to see if I can catch a sight of her. Living next door to someone, you would be surprised at how infrequently you actually bump into them. Though I guess it's best, Shannon doesn't speak to me anymore, the few times we have bumped into each other she just puts her head down and walks on. It's sad, we were best friends for so long, we shared so many great memories. I guess me not staying with Gregg was too much to her, I don't know why, though it left the door open for her and she now spends more time with him than I ever did. Gregg doesn't contact me at all, neither do his family. That's just fine, I don't need them or want them in my life. Shannon is welcome to him though I don't know if anything is going on with them but it looks like it. I still hope Shannon is happy, regardless of everything part of me still loves her. I wish sometimes I could just walk on into her house like old times and have a cup of her perfectly made tea.

I don't feel like I'm where I want to be in life just yet but as the Canvas on my Mum's wall says, "Life is a journey, not a destination." Our home is an actual home now, Mum isn't as crazy about clutter, she still cleans religiously but she's added so many personal touches to the place that we never had before. Her prized possession is now an oversized photo of the two of us, taken by Auntie Orla on my birthday. My Mum and I are laughing and smiling, the camera caught us at a perfect moment. It sums my Mum and I up; best friends. I would never be the person I am today without her, she's my hero. We're a duo now, sticking together through everything, people judge us, give us looks, we laugh them off.

The front door opens and a familiar sound snaps me out of my silence and reflection. The silence of a home without children is amazing yes but the sound of a home with children is the most beautiful sound in the world.

"She wouldn't settle Faith," I smile to myself. "She's maybe hungry I'll give her a feed." I give Addison a soft peck on the lips and look down at our beautiful bundle of joy. I'm not where I want to be in life but I'm certainly not where I was. I lift my little girl into my arms, she's just over a month old but she can certainly scream. When she's in my arms though she settles, I gaze down into her perfect little eyes, so innocent from the world and all that it holds. Knowing that I gave life to my little Anna-Mae is a feeling I could never put into words, I couldn't even begin to. Addison and I joke that she's Mommy and I'm Mummy, my Mum hates being called Granny so she jokes that she'll be Ma.

I look at Addison, she's stressed out, she gets like that when she can't get her settled and Mum and I laugh at her. We tell her it's because she doesn't understand her American accent so she's been practicing her Belfast. It makes me cringe and laugh until tears stream from my eyes. I can't believe the love I feel for her, sometimes I need to pinch myself to believe that it's real. She's my one and only. There's never been so much love under one roof, the four of us wake everyday with a smile and close our eyes much the same.

It feels like only yesterday I was lying in the hospital bed about to give birth. To be honest I completely underestimated how much bringing a life into this world changes someone. I only wish Gregg had felt the same, foolishly I begged him to come and see our little bundle of joy but he wanted nothing to do with us. It's sad really, I can't ever imagine a day without her and I can't comprehend how anyone could know they have a child out there somewhere and make no attempts to be a part of that little person's life. Still, I know my wee baby will be no worse off, she has Addison, my Mum and I. I guess it's true, 'A woman needs a man like a fish needs a bicycle.'

Life is just beginning for all of us, a new lease of an amazing life that I hope nothing will ever take away.

www.excaliburpress.co.uk/store/products

www.ingramcontent.com/pod-product-compliance
Lightning Source LLC
Chambersburg PA
CBHW060932180626
46817CB00004B/1500